SCATTERED MIND

A Descent Into Madness

Table of Contents

Whispers of the Unseen -2
The Watching Eyes -12
Fractured Reflections -22
Don't Look Too Long -29
It Spoke First- 38
Not Alone -47
Torn Between Worlds -65
The Unseen Forces -77
Unraveling Threads -84
Trapped Between Pages -91
If You Lie to Me Again...-162
If You Leave, I'll Break-180
Against the Current-196
Stay With Me-253
The Final Page-288

The Space Between Us-270
Desperate and emotional-213
I Know You're There -99
Stop Reading. See What Happens. -108
Turn Back. Now. -112
You See Me, Don't You? -121
Tell Me I'm Real -132
What's Left of Me? -138
I'm Not Saying That, but the Book Won't Close-226
Not Just a Story-240
We Shouldn't Feel This -143
Stay Until the Pages End-259

One Last Chance-276
The Pages Keep Turning-250
I Shouldn't Want This-147
If You Don't Stop Me... This Can't Be Real-153
Can You Hear Them Too? -174
Lost Without You-190
Kiss Me, Then Run-200
The Shadows Know Your Name-208
Stop Reading. Stop Watching. Stop.-218
Whispers Between the Lines-231
Kiss Me Before We Disappear-246
One Last Chance-276

WHISPERS OF THE UNSEEN

The morning unfolded just like any other.

The refrigerator's hum filled the quiet kitchen, steady and rhythmic, a sound so familiar it blended into the background. A soft breeze pushed through the barely open window, ruffling the edge of a forgotten receipt on the counter. The coffee maker gurgled, filling the air with the bitter scent of brewing caffeine. The world outside was waking up—cars rolling by in the distance, a muffled voice from a passing pedestrian, the occasional chirp of birds perched on the telephone wires.

Everything was **normal.**

Anastasia sat at the table, phone in hand, thumb idly scrolling through news headlines they weren't reading. Their free hand tapped against the ceramic mug in front of them, the dull clink-clink-clink of their fingernail against the surface creating a quiet rhythm. Routine. Predictable.

Then, for just a second, **it happened.**

The air seemed to shift—**just slightly.** A strange weight settled around them, pressing at the edges of their awareness. The kind of sensation that made the tiny hairs on the back of their neck stand up. A whisper of something just out of reach, like walking into a room and immediately forgetting what you came for.

They stopped scrolling.

Their eyes flicked up from the screen, scanning the room. Everything was exactly where it should be—the same messy stack of unopened mail, the same half-empty water bottle left from the night before. Nothing had moved. And yet...

The silence felt **wrong.**

Not total silence—there was still the fridge hum, the faint sound of the coffee pot—but something was **missing.** Like a noise that should have been there had been plucked out of existence, leaving behind a space where it once belonged.

A soft rustling.

The sound was so faint they almost convinced themselves it wasn't real. Like paper shifting, or fabric brushing against itself. It came from nowhere and everywhere all at once, as if the walls themselves had inhaled, just for a moment.

Their gaze flickered to the window, half expecting to see someone standing there. Watching.

Nothing.

A slow exhale. Their fingers, gripping the phone a little tighter than before, relaxed. **I need more sleep.**

The coffee maker beeped, breaking the tension. The moment passed, slipping through their fingers like smoke.

The coffee was too bitter.

Anastasia frowned as they took another sip, their tongue recoiling at the sharpness of it. Had they forgotten the sugar? They could've sworn they'd added some. Another glance at the counter. The sugar jar sat right where it always did, the lid slightly askew like they had just used it.

Strange.

They swirled the coffee absentmindedly, watching the liquid spiral, dark and endless. Maybe their mind was just playing tricks. **It was early. They were tired. That was all.**

Phone in hand, they checked the time. **7:42 AM.**

Wait. No, that couldn't be right.

They were sure it had been **7:42 AM** a minute ago. Maybe longer. Their eyes flicked to the microwave clock. **7:42 AM.** The stove clock. **7:42 AM.**

The phone screen dimmed, reflecting their face at them. A still frame of someone trying not to feel ridiculous. The logical part of their brain was already explaining it away—maybe the clocks weren't synced right, maybe their phone had frozen for a second. Simple things. Stupid things.

Still, their fingers hesitated before refreshing the screen.

7:43 AM.

A quiet laugh pushed past their lips. See? Nothing weird. Just their brain making something out of nothing.

The day moved on. Breakfast. Shower. The usual routine, a familiar rhythm that should have grounded them. And yet, **the feeling never fully left.** That strange sense of being slightly out of sync, like they were a half-second behind reality.

At one point, as they were brushing their teeth, something shifted in the mirror.

A flicker.

Not their reflection. No, that was normal. It was... something else. Like the mirror had lagged, like for a fraction of a second it had shown something different before catching up. But when they leaned closer, eyes scanning every inch of the glass, there was only them.

The toothbrush trembled slightly in their grip.

It was nothing.

Right?

They turned away, shaking their head, trying to push away the ridiculous thought that something—**someone**—had been there, watching through the glass.

The clock continued ticking forward. The minutes passed. The feeling remained.

And outside, beyond the window, something watched.

Fresh air. That's what she needed.

The walls of her apartment had started to feel too small, pressing in around her like a slow, invisible force. It was irrational, of course. The room was the same size it had always been. And yet, the longer she stayed inside, the heavier the air felt—thick, suffocating.

She needed to get out.

Pulling on her jacket, she muttered to herself, "Just a quick walk. Clear my head. That's all."

Her voice was small in the stillness of the apartment, but it was comforting. Talking to herself had always been a habit, a way to fill the silence when it became too loud.

Stepping outside, she inhaled deeply, letting the crisp morning air fill her lungs. The scent of damp pavement and faint traces of car exhaust mixed with the cold breeze. It smelled like the world waking up.

"See? Fresh air. Not losing it."

The street stretched ahead, familiar and quiet. The pavement was uneven in places, worn from years of use, and the houses lining the road stood still in the soft gray light of the morning. A cat sat lazily on a porch railing, flicking its tail as it watched her pass.

She sighed, rubbing a hand over her face. "You're fine. You're just tired."

But even as she said it, something in her chest tightened.

She could feel it again. That strange, creeping sensation.

Like the world was watching.

She walked faster, focusing on the sound of her footsteps. Everything was normal. She needed to stop being weird about this.

Then—

Flicker.

She froze mid-step.

The streetlamp above her pulsed, a sharp, unnatural flicker that sent a ripple of static through the air.

"...Okay, that was weird," she muttered.

She glanced over her shoulder. The lamp behind her burned steadily, unwavering. Just this one had flickered.

Swallowing, she shook her head. "It's just old wiring." Her voice was quieter this time, but she needed to say it out loud, needed to hear it.

Still, she hesitated before taking another step.

The next streetlamp was only a few feet ahead. She kept her eyes forward, walking beneath it—

Flicker.

Her breath hitched.

She came to a stop again, her fingers curling into fists inside her jacket pockets. Slowly, her head turned.

The street behind her stretched long and empty. The lamps stood still. No one was there.

"...Okay," she said, exhaling slowly. "That's... fine. That's fine."

She was not going to freak out over some stupid lights. It was a coincidence. That was all.

So, she kept walking.

And then—

Footsteps.

Soft. Almost too soft to hear. But they were there.

She stopped walking.

The sound stopped too.

Her mouth went dry. Her pulse hammered against her ribs.

"...Hello?" Her voice barely made it past her lips, but the silence that followed was too sharp. Too aware.

She swallowed hard, turning her head.

The street was empty.

Her throat felt tight. It was nothing. An echo. Maybe she was just hearing her footsteps bouncing off the buildings.

She let out a slow breath, forcing a laugh. "Jesus, you need sleep."

Just to prove herself wrong, she took another step—

Step.

Her stomach twisted.

Another step.

Step.

Her breath caught.

She spun around—no one was there.

The street behind her was still and empty, stretching into the distance with no sign of movement.

Her fingers clenched around the fabric of her jacket. She could hear her breathing, uneven now, too fast.

"...Yeah, no," she muttered. "We're done with the walk."

Her legs moved before she could think, carrying her faster down the sidewalk.

She just needed to get home. That was it. Home. A shower. Coffee. Maybe a full night of sleep for once in her life.

The park entrance was just ahead, the path winding through tall trees swaying gently in the breeze. She could sit for a minute, catch her breath, and shake this ridiculous paranoia.

The further she walked, the quieter it became.

Too quiet.

The usual sounds—chirping birds, the distant hum of cars—had faded. Now, only the wind remained, whispering through the branches.

A chill crawled down her spine.

She turned her head slightly, just enough to glance at the trees.

That's when she saw it.

A figure.

Not moving. Just standing there.

Half-hidden between the trunks, just at the edge of her vision. Unmoving.

Watching.

Her throat tightened. "What the—?"

She blinked.

Gone.

She let out a shaky breath, whipping her head around, and scanning the trees. Nothing. No sign anyone had been standing there at all.

Her heart slammed against her ribs.

"...Okay. That's enough outside for today."

She turned on her heel, walking faster—almost running now, her breath unsteady.

But the feeling didn't leave.

If anything, it got worse.

Because she knew, deep down, she hadn't imagined it.

And whoever had been watching her...

They were getting closer.

The Watching Eyes

The walk home should have been simple.

Just a few turns, a few minutes, and she'd be back in the safety of her apartment, surrounded by walls that—until now—had never felt suffocating.

But something was **off.**

She felt it the moment she left the park. The way the air pressed against her skin, was heavier than before. The way her footsteps echoed just a little too long, like something **else** was stepping right behind her.

She didn't want to turn around.

Didn't want to see it.

"Okay, **calm down**," she muttered to herself, hands shoved deep into her jacket pockets. "You're just tired. That's all. You're just freaking yourself out. It's nothing."

But the feeling didn't go away.

It grew stronger.

The closer she got home, the more it seemed like something was there with her—like someone was waiting.

"Am I... being followed?" She said it out loud, but the words didn't sound like they were hers. It felt like a voice that wasn't hers, one she didn't want to acknowledge.

She quickened her pace, hoping that the faster she walked, the faster the feeling would fade. But it didn't. It clung to her, wrapping around her, almost like it was part of her now.

By the time she reached her apartment building, she was nearly running. The front door slammed shut behind her with a force that echoed through the empty hall.

She fumbled with the lock, her hands shaking. "It's fine. Everything's fine. Just breathe."

Click. The door was secure.

She stepped inside, letting the quiet of the apartment envelop her. The familiar sights—the soft glow of the kitchen light, the half-drunk coffee mug, the blanket thrown across the couch—should have been comforting. **But something was wrong.**

It felt too still.

She stood there for a moment, forcing herself to breathe slowly. "It's nothing. Nothing. You're just tired. You're imagining things."

But even as she said the words, she didn't believe them.

Her eyes flicked nervously around the room. Everything was as it should be. The same dull hum of the refrigerator. The same books are stacked on the counter. Everything is in its place.

But still...

Her eyes drifted to the hallway mirror.

"Don't be stupid. You're being ridiculous." She muttered it to herself, but her feet seemed to move on their own. She couldn't help it—she had to look.

She stepped closer, studying her reflection. The same messy hair. The same tired eyes. Nothing unusual.

Yet...

Her chest tightened. She couldn't explain it, but something about the mirror felt wrong.

"God, what is wrong with me today?" Her voice was thin, and brittle, as she leaned in closer to the glass. "Nothing's out of place. Nothing's... off."

But as she stared at her reflection, she couldn't shake the feeling that **something was waiting.**

She stepped back, about to laugh it off—when suddenly, the lights above her flickered.

She froze.

"No. No, no, no, this is just a light." She shook her head, trying to dismiss the chill running up her spine. "Just a faulty bulb. You're not crazy."

But her reflection wasn't moving with her anymore.

It wasn't.

Her reflection had **stayed.**

Her real body turned, but the reflection—**the other her**—stayed still.

Her stomach lurched.

"I—what the hell?" Her voice came out in a tight whisper, barely audible. Her breath quickened. Her reflection... didn't move.

This wasn't right.

She felt her feet dragging her closer to the mirror, unable to stop herself. "This is... This is crazy. It's just a reflection, right?" Her voice trembled as she spoke, trying to convince herself and trying to force the words to make sense.

And then—

Her reflection **smiled.**

Her heart stopped.

The smile wasn't hers. It was **wrong.**

"I'm—" Her breath caught in her throat. She was paralyzed, unable to move, unable to look away. "What the hell is happening?"

The smile deepened. The thing in the mirror smiled first. Not her.

She wasn't smiling.

But the reflection—**it was watching.**

She stumbled back from the mirror, her pulse pounding in her ears, and for one terrifying second, she couldn't move.

It wasn't real. It couldn't be real.

But everything inside her screamed that it was.

Her hands were shaking so violently that it took her a moment to tear her gaze away from the mirror. She turned quickly, nearly tripping over her feet, and stumbled toward her bedroom.

Don't look back.

But she did.

She couldn't help it. Her eyes flicked back toward the mirror, just a glance, just to make sure the reflection was still the same.

It was.

It was back to normal now. The reflection was just...
her.

But she wasn't convinced.

The smile wasn't something she could shake.

The feeling of being watched... hadn't gone away.

It had only just begun.

FRACTURED REFLECTIONS

She didn't sleep.

She couldn't.

Even after she had slammed the bedroom door shut, shoved a chair under the handle, and buried herself under the covers like a child, the feeling didn't leave.

Something was watching her.

Every time she closed her eyes, she could still see that smile.

By the time morning arrived, her body felt like it had been wrung dry. Her head ached, her throat was tight, and she could barely keep her hands steady as she reached for her phone.

She needed to get out.

Mom and Dad.

They were safe. They were normal. They'd tell her everything was okay.

The drive to her parents' house felt longer than usual.

The roads blurred together, and she wasn't sure if it was from exhaustion or the creeping paranoia in her chest. Every time she stopped at a red light, she found herself checking the rearview mirror, half-expecting to see something wrong.

But there was nothing.

At least, nothing she could see.

By the time she pulled into the driveway, her breath came a little easier. The house was the same—warm, and familiar, the porch light still flickering from when Dad refused to change the bulb.

She gripped the steering wheel tightly. "You're safe," she whispered to herself. "You're fine. Mom and Dad will know what to do."

She got out and knocked.

A few seconds later, the door swung open.

"Sweetheart!" Her mom's voice was too bright, too normal as if the world hadn't tilted on its axis. "This is a surprise! We weren't expecting you."

"I—" She swallowed, suddenly unsure what to say. "I just... needed to see you guys."

Her dad appeared behind her mother, brow furrowed. "Everything alright?"

No.

Not even a little.

She forced herself to step inside, rubbing her arms as if the warmth of their home could chase away the lingering cold clinging to her skin.

She didn't know how to start.

She didn't even know if she should.

But the words tumbled out before she could stop them.

"Something's wrong."

Her parents exchanged a glance. "What do you mean, sweetheart?" her mom asked, leading her toward the couch.

She sat down stiffly, fingers digging into her sleeves. Her voice came out in a whisper.

"I think... I think I'm being watched."

Silence.

Her dad sighed, rubbing the bridge of his nose. "Is this about your apartment? We've told you before, if you don't feel safe, you can—"

"No," she interrupted, shaking her head. "It's not like that. It's not someone outside. It's... it's different."

Her mother frowned. "Different how?"

She hesitated, staring down at her hands.

If she said it out loud, would it make it real?

Would it make her sound crazy?

She inhaled sharply. "Last night, I looked in the mirror, and—" She stopped herself, forcing a bitter laugh. "You know what? Forget it. It sounds stupid."

Her mom reached for her hand. "Honey, what happened?"

She exhaled.

Fine. Fine.

"I looked in the mirror, and..." She swallowed hard, the words barely making it past her lips. "My reflection didn't move. It just—stood there. And then it—" She clenched her jaw, forcing herself to say it.

"It smiled."

A heavy silence filled the room.

Then—

"Honey." Her mother's voice was gentle, too gentle. "You've been working too hard. You said you haven't been sleeping well, right? Maybe you just imagined it."

Her heart sank.

"I didn't imagine it."

Her dad gave her a pointed look. "Sweetie, reflections don't just... stay still. That's not how mirrors work."

I know that! she wanted to scream. Do you think I don't know that?

She clenched her fists. "I know what I saw."

Her mom sighed, rubbing her shoulder. "Maybe you should stay here for a few nights. Get some rest. Reset your mind a bit."

They didn't believe her.

Of course, they didn't.

She wanted to argue, to make them understand, but the words wouldn't come. Instead, she nodded weakly.

"Yeah. That... might be a good idea."

But deep down, she knew.

It wouldn't matter where she stayed.

The watching eyes... would follow.

And the mirror wasn't done with her yet.

28

DON'T LOOK TOO LONG

Her mother had always said she spent too much time looking in the mirror.

Now, she was terrified too.

It had been a full day since the incident at her apartment. A full day of avoiding her reflection, of **pretending** everything was fine under her parents' watchful eyes.

She played along. Smiled at dinner. Let her mom fuss over her. Laughed when her dad cracked his usual dry jokes.

But none of it changed the truth.

The second she was alone—when the sun dipped past the horizon and shadows stretched long across the walls—the feeling returned.

She was being watched.

Even now, standing in the dimly lit bathroom, she could feel it. The weight of unseen eyes pressed against her back.

Her hands trembled as she reached for the faucet, splashing cold water onto her face. **Deep breath. In. Out.**

"You're fine," she whispered. "Nothing happened. It was just... just a trick of the light. Or exhaustion. Or something."

She forced herself to look up.

The mirror was normal.

Her reflection, damp strands of hair sticking to her forehead, stared back.

The longer she held its gaze, the more she expected **something** to be wrong. A shift. A flicker. A smile that wasn't hers.

But nothing happened.

She let out a shaky breath. "See? You're just freaking out over nothing."

A nervous laugh bubbled from her lips. God, she felt ridiculous. It was just her imagination playing tricks on her. **It had to be.**

Still...

As she reached for the towel, she hesitated.

Something felt... off.

She couldn't pinpoint it—just a nagging sensation in her gut, an unshakable wrongness clinging to the air.

Slowly, she turned her head to the side.

Her reflection did the same.

Slow. Deliberate.

Perfectly mirrored.

But something was different.

Her breath caught in her throat as she scanned every detail—the angle of her shoulders, the way her hair clung to damp skin, the slight rise and fall of her chest.

Nothing was wrong.

And yet, **everything was.**

Because of her reflection's eyes...

They weren't looking at her.

They were looking **past** her.

At something behind her.

A cold shiver ran down her spine. She felt her limbs lock, muscles seizing with dread. **No. No, no, no.**

Her breathing turned shallow.

She didn't want to turn around.

She had to.

But she **didn't want to.**

Her fingers clenched the edge of the sink, knuckles going white. "It's not real," she whispered, barely able to hear her voice over the pounding of her heart.

She forced herself to move.

One inch. Then another.

She turned.

The bathroom was empty.

Nothing there.

Nothing there.

Her lungs ached as she exhaled, knees nearly buckling in relief. "Jesus Christ..." she breathed, pressing a shaking hand to her chest. "You need to get a grip."

She turned back to the mirror—

Her reflection hadn't moved.

She froze.

Her stomach twisted in a way that made her want to retch.

She was facing forward again. **But the other her... wasn't.**

Her reflection was still **turned away.**

Still looking behind her.

As if something was **still there.**
33

Her body refused to move. Every instinct screamed at her to run, to break the mirror, to **do something.**

But all she could do was stare.

Don't look too long.

The thought came unbidden, like a whisper curling in the back of her mind.

Don't look too long.

Or it might look back.

She squeezed her eyes shut, forcing herself to breathe. When she opened them again—

Her reflection was normal.

Back in place. Staring at her.

Like nothing had happened.

A sharp knock on the door nearly sent her heart through her ribs.

"Sweetheart?" Her mother's voice. "You okay in there?"

She swallowed, her throat dry. "Y-yeah. I'm fine."

A pause.

"Well, get some sleep, alright?"

"Yeah... yeah, okay."

Footsteps retreated down the hall.

She stayed rooted in place.

Watching herself.

Waiting.

When nothing happened, she finally shut off the light and left the bathroom, **forcing herself not to glance back.**

Even as she climbed into bed, pulling the covers tightly around her, she couldn't shake the feeling.

The feeling that, somewhere, behind the glass, **something was still watching.**

And next time...

It wouldn't just stay behind the mirror.

A loud bang jolted her awake.

Her heart slammed against her ribs as she shot upright, breath coming in short, panicked gasps.

"What the hell...?" she whispered into the darkness.

Another sound followed—a deep, dragging scrape against the floor.

Right outside her bedroom door.

She stared at the wooden frame, her pulse roaring in her ears. The hallway was pitch-black beyond the gap under the door, but something moved. A shifting shadow, slow and deliberate.

"Mom?" Her voice barely made it past her lips.

No answer.

She grabbed her phone from the nightstand, thumb fumbling to turn on the flashlight. The weak glow did little to chase away the shadows.

Another bang. Closer this time.

Her fingers tightened around the blanket. "Dad?"

Silence.

Then—

Creeeeaak.

The floorboard outside her door groaned.

Her stomach twisted into knots. Someone was right there.

She swallowed hard, forcing herself to move. She slid out of bed slowly, her bare feet barely making a sound against the floor. Step by step, she crept toward the door, every breath feeling too loud in the silence.

Her hand hovered over the doorknob.

Maybe it was her dad getting water. Maybe the old wooden floors were just settling.

Then, from the other side of the door—

A whisper.

Low. Crooked. Not her father's voice.

"...I see you."

IT SPOKE FIRST

For a long, breathless moment, she did nothing.

The whisper curled under the door, seeping into the air like damp rot. **"…I SEE YOU."**

Her skin prickled. Her lungs felt tight. **That wasn't her father's voice.**

It wasn't anyone she knew.

She pressed herself against the wall beside the door, gripping the phone in her shaking hands. The flashlight flickered as her thumb hovered over the screen. She could call someone. She could scream.

But she didn't.

She **couldn't.**

Another creak. The shadow behind the door shifted.

A slow, dragging movement. As if whoever—or whatever—it was, was **leaning closer.**

Her breath hitched. "Mom?" she tried again, barely above a whisper.

Silence.

Then—**knock, knock.**

Two soft taps against the wood.

A cold shiver licked up her spine.

It wants me to open it.

The thought came unbidden, slithering into her mind like a warning. Like something instinctual.

She squeezed her eyes shut, forcing her body to stay still. **If I don't move, if I don't answer, maybe it'll go away.**

Maybe.

Another knock. **Louder.**

Her hands trembled as she clutched her blanket, the warmth of the fabric useless against the chill that had settled deep into her bones.

Then—

The doorknob twisted.

A sharp gasp caught in her throat. She scrambled back against the bed, pulse hammering against her ribs. **It was trying to come in.**

The handle jerked once. Twice. Then... stillness.

The air was thick with a waiting, expectant silence.

And then—

"WHY WON'T YOU LET ME IN?"

The voice slithered through the wood, closer now. **Too close.** It wasn't loud, but something about it **dug** into her skin, curling around her spine like an icy tendril.

It wasn't right.

It didn't sound human.

It was **too smooth. Too careful.** Like it was trying to be human, but didn't quite know how.

She clamped a hand over her mouth, heart hammering so hard it hurt.

Don't answer. Don't make a sound.

A long pause. Then—

The knob twisted **all the way.**

The door **creaked open.**

Just an inch. Just enough for the darkness to seep in.

A breath of cold air slithered through the gap, curling against her skin.

And in the sliver of blackness, **something moved.**

She saw the barest glimpse—a shape, a figure. **Too tall. Too thin. Too wrong.**

It shifted slightly, its form stretching into something unnatural, something that didn't fit in the space it occupied.

And then—

It smiled.

A wide, unnatural grin. **Too many teeth.**

Her breath shattered.

Run.

The thought slammed into her like a gunshot.

She lunged for the lamp, fingers fumbling against the switch. The moment the room flooded with light—

The door was shut.

Sealed.

Like it had never been opened at all.

She gasped for breath, vision blurring. The room was **empty.**

But the whisper was still in her head.

Soft. **Patient.**

"You spoke first."

And she knew, with a bone-deep certainty, that it wasn't finished with her yet.

The rest of the day passed in a blur.

She barely ate. Barely spoke. The walls of the house felt **tighter** than usual, the air heavier.

Every shadow seemed **too dark.** Every reflection lingered a second too long.

And then there were **the voices.**

Not loud. Not clear.

But **there.**

Soft, whispering things that curled just beneath the surface of sound—**behind her when she turned a corner, at the edges of her hearing when she tried to focus.**

They weren't **words.** Not really.

More like the **idea** of words.

Like someone was just about to speak... but never did.

By nightfall, her nerves were frayed raw.

She climbed into bed, staring at the ceiling, her body buzzing with exhaustion, but her mind **refused** to rest.

She needed sleep. Just a little.

Just a little.

Her eyes fluttered shut.

Silence.

Then—

Creak.

Her breath caught.

The closet door had moved.

Just an inch.

A sliver of blackness stared back at her.

Her body locked up.

She hadn't touched it. She **knew** she hadn't touched it.

It wasn't open before.

Right?

Right?

Her pulse roared in her ears.

And then—

A whisper.

Low. Almost **gentle.**

But it didn't come from the closet.

It came from the bed.

From right beside her.

Her breath turned shallow. **No. No, no, no.**

She didn't want to turn her head.

She **had** to.

Slowly—so, so slowly—she shifted her gaze.

And in the dim glow of the streetlight filtering through the window...

She saw it.

A shape.

A figure curled under the blankets, lying **right beside her.**

Not moving.

Just... **waiting.**

A sob built in her throat. Her hands clenched the sheets, her fingers trembling.

And then—

It **smiled.**

A wide, too-white grin.

And it spoke.

"...YOU LET ME IN."

NOT ALONE

The evening sky outside had darkened into deep shades of violet and indigo. Anastasia sat in the corner of her room, the dim light from her desk lamp casting long shadows across the walls. The pages of the book in her lap were no longer holding her attention, her eyes wandering, lost in thought. The words seemed to blur, as though the letters themselves were trying to escape from her mind.

She had always been a night owl, but tonight felt different. The silence in the room was heavy, and oppressive, as if the air itself were holding its breath. And it was then that she first noticed it—a strange, almost imperceptible sensation at the back of her neck.

A shiver.

Anastasia blinked and straightened up in her chair, her fingers still resting on the book's pages. Her gaze flicked toward the door, then the window. Everything was exactly where it should be, untouched. The room, as she had left it, was still and quiet.

It's nothing, she told herself, shaking her head to clear the thought. *Just the wind. Probably.*

She tried to refocus on her book, but the feeling refused to leave. The soft hum of the evening air whispered through the cracks in the window, the only sound that broke the heavy silence. Her heart rate had picked up, though she couldn't quite explain why.

Her eyes darted around the room once more, a quick sweep over the furniture and the open closet door. Everything was normal, but that sensation... It clung to her like a shadow, pressing closer, suffocating her with its weight.

Then she heard it.

A faint creak from behind her. So quiet she almost convinced herself it had been her imagination. But no. There it was again—a subtle, almost inaudible sound, like a floorboard groaning under someone's weight.

Anastasia's heart skipped a beat. She slowly turned her head, her body tense, her breath caught in her throat.

"Hello?" she called out, her voice shaky, betraying the calm she tried to project. She swallowed hard, glancing over her shoulder. "Is anyone there?"

The room was still. The air was thick with silence.

She let out a breath she didn't realize she was holding, chalking it up to nerves. *You're being paranoid,* she thought. *It's just the house settling.*

But as she stood up, a feeling settled over her like a dark cloud. She could feel it now—a pressure in the air, something unseen, watching her. The shadows in the corners of the room seemed to deepen, as though the darkness itself was reaching out.

"Get it together, Ana," she muttered, shaking her head and walking toward the window, hoping the cool breeze outside would calm her racing thoughts.

As her fingers brushed the curtain, the unease in her chest grew. The trees outside the window swayed gently in the wind, but the quiet rustle was drowned out by a strange, oppressive silence inside the room. She stopped herself mid-motion, her fingers trembling slightly as she pulled back the curtain just enough to peer out.

Nothing. The yard was empty. The distant hum of streetlights flickered quietly in the distance.

Still, something felt wrong.

I'm being silly, she told herself again. *No one's here. You're imagining things.*

Just as she was about to pull away from the window, she heard it again. This time, the creak was louder, unmistakable.

Her breath hitched.

It came from the closet.

Her legs froze, and her heart thundered in her chest. She knew she had closed that door earlier. She was sure of it.

"Who's there?" she asked, her voice barely above a whisper. She swallowed hard, gathering the courage to walk toward the closet. Every step felt like it was echoing in the stillness of the room, the sound unnervingly loud.

She reached the door, hesitating for a moment before she slowly turned the handle. The door creaked open, revealing the dark interior of the closet.

Empty.

Her shoulders slumped in relief, though her mind still couldn't shake the unease. She stepped back, but before she could turn away, something caught her eye. A faint movement, almost imperceptible, at the edge of the room.

She spun around, her breath catching in her throat. The air was thick now, oppressive, and she could feel her pulse racing.

"Who's there?" she called out again, her voice stronger now, tinged with both fear and anger. "This isn't funny anymore."

No response. Only the eerie stillness, the silence that seemed to stretch on forever.

Then, from the corner of the room, a whisper—a soft, barely audible breath against the silence.

Not alone.

Anastasia's heart pounded in her chest as the whisper from the corner of the room lingered in the air. The words seemed to hang like a cold mist, impossible to ignore.

Not alone.

Her hands trembled as she gripped the edge of the closet door, her mind racing. She had to tell someone—anyone. She wasn't imagining this. Something was happening. Someone was watching her.

With a sudden rush of determination, she turned and fled down the hallway. Her breath came in short, frantic bursts as she made her way to the living room. Her parents were sitting on the couch, absorbed in their usual evening routine—her mother flipping through a magazine, her father clicking through channels on the TV.

"Mom! Dad!" Anastasia's voice was sharp, strained. She nearly collapsed onto the couch beside them, grabbing their attention in an instant.

Both of her parents turned to look at her, their expressions confused, yet tinged with concern.

"What's wrong, sweetie?" her mother asked, setting the magazine aside.

Anastasia could barely contain the urgency in her voice as she blurted out, "I swear someone's been watching me. I—there's something in the house, I know it. I keep feeling it. I'm not imagining it. I'm not crazy!"

Her father frowned, setting the remote down and adjusting his glasses. "Ana, calm down. What are you talking about? You've been fine all week."

"I'm not fine! You don't understand! The room feels—there's a presence, like... like someone is there, even when no one is." Her voice quivered with desperation. "I'm scared, Mom. Please, I need you to believe me."

Her mother's face softened, but there was a flicker of uncertainty in her eyes. "Honey, I think you're just overstressed. It's been a lot lately with school, and I know things haven't been easy—"

"I'm not imagining it, Mom!" Anastasia interrupted, shaking her head fiercely. "I feel it. I hear things. Someone's watching me, and I don't know who or why. I don't know what's happening, but it's real!"

Her father's gaze turned more serious, but not in the way she had hoped. "Ana, you've been having a rough time lately. You've been talking about things that don't make sense, and now this... this paranoia? I think you might be dealing with more than just stress. Maybe it's time we took you to see someone."

Anastasia recoiled, her heart sinking. "What? No! I don't need therapy, I need help! I need you to believe me!"

Her mother exchanged a glance with her father, and then, to Anastasia's horror, they both stood up. Her father spoke with a quiet but firm tone. "Ana, we're worried about you. We think it's best if we take you to see a doctor. You've been saying strange things, and we need to figure out what's going on with you."

Anastasia's breath hitched in her throat. "No... no! I don't need to see a doctor! I'm fine! I'm telling you the truth!"

But her parents weren't listening anymore. Her father, looking stern, walked toward the phone, dialing quickly. "I'm calling a professional. You need help, Anastasia."

"No!" She felt panic rising in her chest. "Don't—don't do this! I'm not crazy!"

Her mother's voice, though gentle, was insistent. "We just want to help you, Ana. We're not saying you're crazy. But this... this isn't normal. You've been talking about being watched, about things that don't make sense. We can't ignore it anymore."

Anastasia shook her head, her hands trembling. "I'm not making it up! I'm not! I swear to you—" Her words were cut off by the sound of her father's voice again, this time more distant, as if he were speaking to someone else.

"We need to take her in, Doctor. I don't know what's going on, but I think she needs to be evaluated."

Anastasia's world seemed to crumble as she heard her father's cold words. She turned to her mother, her eyes wide with disbelief. "Please... Mom, please! You don't believe me? You think I'm crazy?"

Her mother's eyes filled with sorrow. "I believe you, Ana. But we need answers. We need to know what's happening, and right now, we don't have them."

Her father nodded grimly. "It's for the best."

The words hit her like a punch to the gut. She felt as though the room was spinning, the walls closing in around her.

"No..." Anastasia whispered, backing away. "I'm fine. Please, I swear I'm fine. I don't need to go to a hospital." Her voice cracked, but the words wouldn't stop coming. "I don't need to be locked up. I'm not... not crazy. I just... I just want to be safe."

Her mother stepped forward, her face twisted in guilt. "I'm sorry, sweetheart. We'll get you the help you need."

Anastasia turned and ran. She bolted for the front door, hands scrabbling at the lock in a frantic attempt to escape. But before she could reach it, her father grabbed her arm, his grip unyielding.

"Ana, please," he said, his voice a mixture of frustration and concern. "Let us help you. This is the only way."

She twisted away, her heart racing as she tried to pull free. "No! I'm not going!"

But in that moment, she felt something cold settle deep within her. The realization hit her with gut-wrenching force: she wasn't just fighting her parents. She was fighting a reality they didn't want to see—a reality that was becoming more and more impossible to ignore.

Before she knew it, she was being led out of the house, her body numb, as her parents drove her to the hospital. No one would believe her. No one would see what she saw.

And in that moment, as the world around her seemed to fall apart, Anastasia knew one terrifying truth:

She was alone.

A Mind Divided

The sterile scent of antiseptic filled the air, mingling with the hum of fluorescent lights overhead. Anastasia sat on the edge of the small hospital bed, her legs dangling loosely in front of her, swinging back and forth in a restless rhythm. The room felt too small, too confining, and yet, it was better than the suffocating feeling of the world outside. Or so she told herself.

She tried to focus on the white walls, the blank canvas that surrounded her, but the silence made it worse. She could still feel the heavy weight of being watched, as though invisible eyes were trained on her from every corner of the room. She gripped the edges of the bed, trying to steady herself, but the dizziness didn't stop.

Maybe it's all in my head.

The thought was there, flickering in the back of her mind, but it wasn't comforting. It didn't make the unease go away. It only made her more terrified that perhaps she had gone mad. What if they were right? What if everything she'd felt—the whispers, the creeping presence—was just a product of her imagination? What if the truth was she wasn't being watched at all?

She squeezed her eyes shut, trying to block out the swirling thoughts, the competing voices in her head. One part of her screamed that something was wrong—*Something is here. It's real. You're not crazy. They don't understand.* But another part whispered doubt—*Maybe you are crazy. What if it's just stress? What if it's just your mind playing tricks on you?*

A knock at the door broke her internal struggle, and she quickly wiped her hands down her face, blinking to clear the haze from her mind.

"Anastasia? It's Dr. Langley," a calm voice called from the other side.

She stood up, feeling the familiar dizziness surge through her body, but managed to steady herself just as the door opened. Dr. Langley, a tall woman in her forties with dark, curly hair, stepped in, holding a clipboard in one hand.

"How are you feeling today?" she asked, her tone professional but not unfriendly.

Anastasia forced a smile, though it felt thin and fragile. "I'm fine. Just... tired."

Dr. Langley raised an eyebrow, her gaze sharp. "I understand. You've been through a lot recently. The hospital environment can be difficult to adjust to, especially when you're under stress. That's why we're here—to help you. To help you make sense of everything."

Anastasia nodded but didn't trust herself to speak. She didn't trust the words that might slip out. The ones that sounded crazy, even to her ears. She glanced toward the window, hoping to avoid Dr. Langley's probing gaze. Outside, the sun had started to set, casting long shadows across the yard.

"You've been telling us you've felt like you're being watched," Dr. Langley said gently, lowering her clipboard. "Can you tell me more about that? When do you feel it the most?"

Anastasia stiffened. She didn't want to explain. She didn't want to sound like a paranoid child. But the pressure in her chest grew, and she knew she had to say something, or they'd just lock her away and write her off as delusional.

"It's... it's all the time," Anastasia whispered. "I feel it in the room. At night, when I'm awake. Sometimes... I hear whispers, but when I look around, there's no one there."

Dr. Langley nodded, jotting something down on her clipboard. "Do you think the whispers are real, or could they be a product of stress? Sometimes, when the mind is under extreme pressure, it can manifest... feelings, sensations, that aren't necessarily there."

"I don't know," Anastasia replied, her voice trembling. She clenched her fists at her sides, trying to hold herself together. "I *feel* it, though. I can't explain it. I don't know how to make it stop."

The doctor's expression softened. "I understand this is hard for you, Anastasia. I'm here to help. But we need to get to the root of what's causing these feelings. You must trust me."

Anastasia swallowed, a lump forming in her throat. "I don't know who to trust anymore. I don't even know if I can trust myself."

For a moment, the room fell silent, the only sound the soft hum of the fluorescent lights above. Dr. Langley's eyes softened, and she placed a hand gently on Anastasia's arm.

"I understand that this feels terrifying," she said, her voice low and comforting. "But you're not alone here. We'll work through this together. But we need you to be open with me. You need to trust that we can help you."

Anastasia shook her head, her hands gripping the bed's edge again. "But what if... what if I *am* crazy?" she muttered, barely above a whisper. "What if it's all in my head? What if I'm just imagining it all?"

Dr. Langley took a deep breath, her eyes searching Anastasia's face as if weighing her words carefully. "Sometimes, the mind can play tricks on us. But that doesn't mean you're crazy. It means something deeper is going on. And we need to figure it out together. But to do that, you have to open up. You have to trust me."

Anastasia looked down at her hands, the weight of Dr. Langley's words pressing down on her. Could she trust her? Could she trust anyone? She felt torn, divided between the part of her that was certain something was wrong and the part that wondered if she was simply losing her grip on reality. Every time she tried to make sense of it all, the truth seemed to slip through her fingers.

"I don't know anymore," she whispered, her voice barely audible. "I'm scared."

Dr. Langley gave her a long, empathetic look. "I know, Anastasia. And I promise, we'll do everything we can to help you find your way through this."

As the doctor left, Anastasia's mind swirled with doubt. She wanted to believe that there was help, that this feeling of being watched would eventually fade, but deep down, she knew something was wrong—something that went beyond what anyone could explain. Her mind felt like a battlefield, torn between two competing truths: the one that said she was losing her mind and the one that told her there was something out there, watching, waiting.

And maybe... just maybe, I'm not crazy.

The thoughts raged within her, as fragmented and contradictory as ever. She couldn't escape the pull of each side—the part that demanded answers, and the part that feared what those answers might be.

In that small hospital room, Anastasia was left alone with her thoughts, caught between reality and delusion, her mind divided, fighting itself.

TORN BETWEEN WORLDS

Anastasia sat on the edge of her bed again, her fingers tracing the cold, rigid edges of the hospital mattress. The sterile room around her felt different today, as though the air itself was charged with something she couldn't name. The hum of the fluorescent lights, usually a constant background noise, seemed to pulse in rhythm with her thoughts. And yet, the more she sat in silence, the more something strange occurred to her—something unsettling.

I'm being watched.

The thought came unbidden, but it wasn't the usual paranoia that had gripped her in the past. No, this was different. This was real. She could feel it. It was as if there was something more than just the invisible eyes of the staff or her supposed delusions. It was... the sense that someone—or something—was observing her, but in a way that felt as if they weren't even trying to hide it.

Her pulse quickened as she turned her head slowly to glance around the room, though she knew no one was physically there. Still, she couldn't shake the sensation of being under scrutiny. Not just from the doctors or her parents or even the whispers of the staff as they passed by outside her door. No, this felt different.

Her mind, already stretched thin, began to make connections that shouldn't have existed. It was as though something beyond her reality was pressing in, something that had no place in her world—a force that was not only watching her but was also *aware* of her thoughts.

Am I imagining this? she thought, clutching the sides of her chair in an attempt to ground herself. But then, something odd happened. She caught herself staring directly at the window across the room, where the blinds were partially drawn. Her reflection looked back at her, but the image seemed... different. Her eyes, wide with a mix of fear and confusion, stared back at her, but there was something wrong.

For a split second, it wasn't just her reflection that was there. There was a flicker—something else. A shadow, a presence that wasn't part of the room.

I know you're out there. The thought wasn't hers, yet it echoed within her mind as if responding to her fear. The words felt like they were being pulled directly from the depths of her thoughts and formed by some unseen force. But how could that be possible?

Her breath caught in her throat. The air felt heavy, charged with the overwhelming realization that she was no longer just trapped within the confines of the hospital walls. No, something much stranger was happening.

She turned to look directly at the wall opposite her. The blankness of the white walls had always been oppressive, but now, they seemed to be... waiting. It was as if the space itself was alive with the anticipation of something—of *someone.*

She suddenly became painfully aware of her voice, her thoughts, and how they seemed to be *reaching out* into the silence of the room. It was as if she were speaking aloud in some way that didn't make sense.

You're reading this, she thought, her mind racing. The words came almost involuntarily. The more she tried to push them back, the more they surged to the forefront. *You're watching me, aren't you?*

It wasn't a question she had intended to ask aloud, but it spilled from her thoughts with startling clarity. She could feel it, the weight of eyes that weren't in the room with her but somehow, were. Watching, waiting, pulling her words from her very mind. She wasn't crazy—this wasn't some delusion. Something or someone was reading her thoughts.

For the first time since all of this began, Anastasia felt as though she had no control over her narrative. She was no longer simply a participant in her own life—she was the subject, the object of observation, an entity in a story where she was not the author.

She wanted to scream, to lash out at the invisible presence that seemed to hover just outside her awareness. But she couldn't. She could only sit there, frozen in place, the realization of being *watched* settling like a cold weight on her chest.

The door to her room creaked open, and Dr. Langley stepped inside, her expression professional but laced with concern.

"How are we feeling today, Anastasia?" she asked, her eyes briefly flicking over to the silent space around them.

Anastasia opened her mouth to respond but found the words stuck in her throat. She didn't know how to explain the sense of intrusion, the invisible audience pressing in on her thoughts. She had to fight to hold onto some semblance of reality, to resist the pull of the feeling that her every move was being dictated, scrutinized by unseen forces.

"I... I think... I think someone is watching me," she said suddenly, the words tumbling out before she could stop them. She looked at Dr. Langley with wide, frantic eyes. "Someone or something...is watching me...."

Dr. Langley's brow furrowed, but her voice remained steady. "Anastasia, we've talked about this. You're under a lot of stress, and we're here to help you work through these feelings. It's important to stay grounded."

Anastasia shook her head vehemently, her heart pounding in her chest. "No, you don't understand! I know... I know they're out there. You can't hear them, but they're listening, they're waiting, they're... reading me!"

Dr. Langley stepped closer, gently placing her hand on Anastasia's shoulder. "I know this is hard, but you need to trust us. We're doing everything we can to help you find the answers, but you have to be willing to work with us. We can't help you if you don't let us."

But Anastasia didn't hear her anymore. She was lost in the overwhelming awareness that she was no longer alone in her mind. That the world she had once controlled, that her thoughts had once been her own, was slipping through her fingers.

She stood up suddenly, her mind racing, trying to make sense of the impossible. There was no escaping the feeling that something was watching her—*waiting for her to figure it out*. She wasn't sure if it was a voice, a presence, or something more, but it was real. It had to be.

For the first time, Anastasia wondered if she was not just trapped in the hospital—but trapped within a story and trapped in a world where the line between what was real and what was imagined had been forever blurred.

And the watchers? They weren't going anywhere.

Anastasia sat on the edge of her bed, her hands clenched tightly together. The oppressive white walls of her room, once so sterile and distant, now seemed to close in on her, as though the space was bending under an invisible pressure. The air was thick, almost suffocating. The hum of the fluorescent lights overhead felt louder today, a constant pulse in the back of her mind, vibrating against her skull.

She couldn't shake the feeling. It had been building for days, growing stronger, more insistent. Every time she closed her eyes, it was there—lurking just beneath the surface of her thoughts. She wasn't just being watched. She *knew* it now.

Her breath hitched, and her fingers twitched with a nervous energy. She couldn't stop it. The feeling was relentless, like a cold hand around her heart, squeezing tighter and tighter. And then, it happened again—the thing she had tried to ignore. The thing she had convinced herself was a delusion.

Her gaze shifted to the corner of the room, where she had seen it before—the feeling that something was... waiting. Her eyes darted around the space, her body tense, as though expecting the presence to manifest itself again. But instead, she found something even more horrifying.

Right there, in the empty corner, she could see it now. It wasn't just the shadows or the faint reflection of her fear. But so vivid, so unmistakably there. She felt eyes crawling onto her skin and watching her.

Her heart pounded in her chest, and she gasped. She blinked rapidly, but the eyes remained, crawling, Moving. She knew it wasn't real—knew it had to be some trick of her mind. But the longer she felt it, the more it felt like it was *watching her*, its unseen gaze crawling over her skin.

No. No, this can't be real. It's just a trick, she thought, but even as she tried to deny it, her mind fought back, forcing the image into sharper focus. It was real. It was there. It was watching her.

Her breath became erratic as the eyes seemed to watch, it started growing larger in her mind. She could almost feel it pressing on her. The walls of the room seemed to spin, and the ground beneath her feet became unstable. She gripped the edge of the bed, her knuckles turning white.

"I'm not crazy. I'm not crazy," she muttered to herself, her voice trembling. "It's real. It's real. Someone's watching me."

Her words echoed in the room, but there was no comfort in them. The more she spoke, the more she began to feel like she was unraveling. Like the space around her was slipping away, warping into something that couldn't possibly exist outside her mind.

Her vision blurred as tears filled her eyes. She squeezed them shut, trying to block out the overwhelming sensation. But when she opened them again, the eyes were like a camera was still there watching me, and she could see it even more clearly. But they seemed to mock her like a cold eye staring into her very soul.

"I can't... I can't do this anymore," Anastasia whispered, her voice cracking. She felt her legs go weak, her body trembling violently. "I don't know what's happening. I don't... I don't know what's real."

A sob caught in her throat, and before she could stop herself, she slid to the floor, her knees buckling under her. The tears came, hot and fast, as her body shook uncontrollably. She couldn't breathe. She couldn't think. All she could do was feel the suffocating presence, the ever-watchful eyes that seemed to pierce through her, judging her every thought, every movement.

"I'm... I'm sorry... please... stop watching me..." she gasped, her words coming out in ragged breaths. She pulled her knees to her chest, trying to make herself small, trying to hide from the unrelenting gaze that loomed over her.

The room seemed to close in on her, and she screamed, the sound tearing through the silence, echoing in her ears. But it didn't matter. Nothing changed. The camera was still there, watching. She wasn't alone. And she would never be alone again.

Later, Dr. Langley arrived.

The door creaked open slowly, and Dr. Langley stepped into the room, her gaze immediately landing on Anastasia curled on the floor, her hands covering her face, her shoulders shaking with sobs.

"Anastasia? Anastasia, can you hear me?" Dr. Langley's voice was calm, and measured, but there was a sharp edge to it now—concern mixing with something darker, more questioning. She knelt beside her, placing a hand on her shoulder.

Anastasia recoiled, pulling away from the touch as though burned. Her wide, frantic eyes locked onto Dr. Langley, and she whimpered.

"Don't touch me!" she cried. "Don't! Can't you see? You're all watching me! *All of you!*"

Dr. Langley's face hardened, but she quickly masked it with professionalism. She spoke softly, as though to a child. "Anastasia, listen to me. You're safe here. There is no camera. No one is watching you like that. You need to calm down. We're going to help you."

Anastasia could barely hear her over the sound of her sobs. The overwhelming sense of being trapped in a reality that was not her own seemed to drown out everything else.

"You don't understand!" she cried out, her voice breaking. "Someone is part of it! *Someone is watching me!*"

Dr. Langley paused, watching her carefully. For a moment, there was a flicker of something in her eyes—something darker, something more knowing. But it was gone in an instant, replaced by a mask of calm professionalism.

"We'll help you through this, Anastasia," Dr. Langley said gently, but there was a coldness to her words now that made Anastasia shiver. "Just trust me. It's all in your head."

But at that moment, Anastasia wasn't so sure anymore. She wasn't so sure what was real, what was imagined, or who—or *what*—was watching her.

THE UNSEEN FORCES

The room felt colder today. Anastasia couldn't explain it—she hadn't seen a single open window or air vent since being brought to the hospital. Yet, the temperature of the air had droppedthe silence heavier.

Her hands trembled as she held the edge of the thin hospital blanket, fingers pressed so hard against the fabric that her knuckles turned white. The oppressive sense of *being watched* was back, stronger than ever. It clawed at her mind, pushing her thoughts into a vortex of panic.

She tried to steady her breath, sucking in the cool air, but it only made her lightheaded. The pressure built in her chest until she thought she might suffocate under the weight of it.

Not again. Please, not again, she begged silently, squeezing her eyes shut. She couldn't escape it. She knew what was coming. The feeling—the sharp, nauseating sensation of being observed—crept into her consciousness, uninvited, relentless.

And then, it happened.

Her eyes snapped open, Her eyes flickered across the room seemingly trying to catch something. Not real, The eyes were still vividly in her mind, its presence so palpable She closed her eyes and she opened and she saw a thing staring at her. She gasped and recoiled as if the very sight of it could burn her. Her breath hitched in her throat, and before she could stop herself, a scream tore through her. It was raw, guttural, and frantic, a primal sound that echoed off the walls.

"*NO!*" she screamed, her voice strangled with panic, her body rigid with terror. She scrambled backward, pressing herself against the wall as if she could somehow escape the suffocating presence of the unseen force.

Tears sprang to her eyes as she clutched her head, trying to block out the invasive image. She squeezed her eyes shut, her face contorted in distress. She was shaking, her entire body trembling as though the very air was crushing her.

"I can't... I can't..." She sobbed, her words barely audible through her sobs. "Please... stop watching me. I... I'm not crazy... please..."

The eternal force, still there in the corner, remained silent, its eyes watching unwavering in its scrutiny. She couldn't stop it. She couldn't hide from it.

The room seemed to close in on her, and she curled into herself, arms wrapped tightly around her knees as she sobbed uncontrollably. *It's real*, she thought desperately. *It's real, and no one believes me.*

Her sobs shook her entire body. The fear was a physical thing, gnawing at her insides, clawing at her heart. She could feel the presence of a heavy weight pressing down on her chest, and every breath felt like a struggle.

Suddenly, the door creaked open, and Dr. Langley's calm voice cut through the chaos of Anastasia's mind. "Anastasia? What's happening?"

Anastasia didn't look up. She couldn't bear to. She only heard her cries filling the room, drowning out all other sounds.

"They're watching me!" she cried out, her voice hoarse, cracked with emotion. "They're watching... always watching..."

Dr. Langley's footsteps approached cautiously, but Anastasia recoiled, clutching her knees tighter to her chest. Her skin felt hot with feverish sweat, and her heart thudded in her ears. She could feel Dr. Langley's presence, but it felt distant, unreal, as if she, too, were part of the observation. Part of the unseen forces that were tormenting her.

"I can't escape it! Please... you don't understand..." Anastasia's words dissolved into more sobs as her vision blurred with tears. "It's not in my head! It's real... *they're real!*"

Dr. Langley paused, her voice softer now, but still professional, as though trying to reach the rational part of Anastasia's mind. "Anastasia, listen to me. This is part of what we need to work through. It's not real, okay? There's no camera. You're safe."

But those words only made the force's presence more insistent. It *was* real. The force was still there, staring at her, watching, judging.

Anastasia's breath came in ragged gasps as she tried to push away the image. She could feel the invisible eyes on her, feel the weight of their presence pressing against her. Her cries became more desperate.

"I'm not crazy! Please!" Her voice was a whisper now, broken and soft, as though speaking too loudly would bring the camera's gaze crashing down on her. Her body shook violently as tears streamed down her face, the fear taking over every inch of her being.

Dr. Langley stepped closer, but Anastasia's eyes widened as she caught a glimpse of the imaginary camera again. This time, it seemed to zoom in on her, its presence more intrusive than ever. She screamed again, the sound ragged and raw.

"No, no, no, no!" she shrieked, her voice breaking under the weight of her panic. She couldn't think. She couldn't breathe. The pressure in her chest felt unbearable.

At that moment, she thought she might break. She thought she might shatter into a thousand pieces, lost in the chaos of her mind. But the eyes didn't stop. It just kept watching me. Just felt like it was tugging at me.

The room felt suffocating, and her sobs echoed through the space, growing louder, more frantic. She pulled her knees tighter to her chest, shaking violently. "Please," she whispered, barely audible. "I can't take this... please..."

Dr. Langley knelt beside her, her voice calm but firm. "Anastasia, you need to breathe. You need to focus on me. There is no monster here. You're safe here."

But Anastasia couldn't hear her. She couldn't see her. All she could see was that thing in the corner, the feeling of eyes upon her, the constant, never-ending sense of being watched, studied, dissected.

And the tears kept coming. They fell like a relentless storm, soaking her cheeks, the salt stinging her skin as her chest heaved in short, broken breaths.

Later

The room was quiet now, the stillness of the hospital room pressing in, suffocating. Anastasia sat at the edge of her bed, her face streaked with tears. Her hands were folded tightly in her lap, knuckles white from the pressure.

She stared at the floor, her gaze unfocused, lost in the haze of exhaustion and fear.

Unraveling Threads

The walls of the hospital room felt like they were pressing in on her, squeezing, collapsing inwards with a force that threatened to crush her entire existence. Anastasia sat in the middle of her bed, her hands clutched tightly together, her fingers white from the pressure. Her breathing was shallow and uneven. The steady beep of the heart monitor was the only thing that reminded her she was still alive. That, and the pressure in her chest—so tight, so suffocating.

But even the rhythmic beep seemed too steady, too predictable, as though everything was scripted. And maybe it was. Maybe none of this was real. Maybe she wasn't even *here* at all. Maybe everything was a show, a performance—one where she was the unwilling star.

She turned her head toward the corner of the room, her eyes darting around. It had become a habit, this constant scanning, looking for something—anything—that would prove she was not alone. She could still feel them, those unseen forces. They were watching, waiting. Watching her every move, every thought.

Her hands began to tremble again, the sensation of being observed swelling in her chest. The force. She saw it again, that cold glare, watching her from the corner. But this time, it wasn't just in the corner. It was everywhere—lurking in the corners of her vision, hanging in the air like a dark cloud.

"They're all watching," she whispered, her voice wavering. "They're all watching me. And you, too. You're watching me, aren't you? I know you are."

Her eyes shifted, locking onto the white tile wall in the corner. It didn't blink, didn't move. Just watched.

"I can feel your eyes on me. *I can feel you*," she said, her voice louder now, strained. "Stop. Stop it. Stop watching me! I—I can't take it anymore."

She rocked back and forth on the bed, her arms hugging her knees to her chest as her breathing became ragged. Her face contorted in agony as the weight of the pressure bore down on her, pushing her further into madness. The walls pressed in closer, and she couldn't tell where her thoughts ended and the room began. Her mind was unraveling, the threads of her reality slipping through her fingers.

"Please, someone help me." She gasped, her voice breaking with desperation. *"I'm not crazy. I'm not crazy, right? You see it too, don't you? You're reading this. You know. You know what I'm going through."*

Her hands shot up to her head, clutching at her hair, trying to stop the world from spinning, from folding in on itself. She screamed. It was a harsh, jagged sound, full of pain and fear. Her entire body tensed, her heart pounding so fast it felt like it was about to explode.

The door opened quietly, and her parents stepped inside.

"Anastasia?" her mother's voice was soft, concerned. But there was an edge to it now, something that sounded almost like an accusation. "We're here. How are you feeling today?"

Anastasia's head snapped toward them. Her eyes were wild and frantic, and her pupils were dilated, giving her a crazed, almost feverish look. She didn't speak at first, just stared at them as if they were part of the twisted show she couldn't escape. She knew they didn't believe her—knew they thought she was losing her mind. They never *saw* it. They never *felt* it the way she did.

"They're watching me," she whispered, her voice hoarse. "Do you see it? The eyes. *It's there.* They're watching us. Watching me."

Her mother stepped closer, her face full of concern, but her eyes betrayed something else. Something colder. Maybe it was fear. Maybe it was doubt.

"Anastasia, honey, you need to calm down," her father said in a tone that was almost too flat, too practiced. "You're having another episode. You're not being watched by anyone. It's just your mind playing tricks on you. You've been through a lot lately, and we're here for you. But you have to trust us. We want to help you."

"Help me?" she snapped, her voice rising. "*Help me?* You don't understand! You don't get it! You're all part of it, aren't you?." Her eyes darted to the window. The reflection of her parents in the glass stared back at her—two blurry figures in the distorted glass. She shook her head violently. "You're not real. None of you are real."

Her parents exchanged a look—one Anastasia could see all too clearly. It was the look they had when they thought she was too far gone when they didn't know how to fix her anymore.

"We can't help you if you don't help yourself, sweetheart," her father said, his voice colder now, a thin thread of frustration creeping into his tone. "You need to stop thinking like this. Stop imagining things that aren't there."

The presents were still there, in the corner of the room. The presence of it pressed down on her chest like a physical weight, squeezing her lungs, suffocating her. She could feel her heart pounding against her ribs. She wanted to scream. To beg them to see it.

She could feel the weight of the eyes on her. She could feel them reading her every word. *You see me,* she thought. *You're all reading me right now, aren't you? Watching me unravel, piece by piece.*

"I'm not crazy," she whispered again, her voice cracking with a raw, broken desperation. "I'm not crazy, I'm not... I'm not crazy..."

Her hands gripped the sides of her head once more as tears began to spill down her face. She didn't want to lose herself. She didn't want to be lost in this world where nothing was real and everything was a lie. But it was happening, and she could feel it happening, each thread of her reality snapping, unraveling, until nothing was left but the dark, empty void.

Her mother stepped forward, her hand trembling as she reached out to touch Anastasia's arm. "Anastasia, please... please listen to us. We want to help. We love you."

Anastasia jerked away violently, her voice rising into a scream. "*I don't want your help!* I just want it to stop. I just want to be *free!*" Her words were a mix of agony and rage, and they felt so foreign to her ears.

Her parents stood there, helpless, watching their daughter spiral further into herself. They couldn't see it. They couldn't see what was happening. They couldn't feel what she felt.

"I'm not crazy," she whispered one last time, the words barely escaping her lips. "Please... make it stop."

But the camera didn't stop. It never stopped.

TRAPPED BETWEEN PAGES

"Name?"

She stared at the clipboard in the nurse's hands. The pen hovered, waiting, expecting.

Her mouth felt dry.

"You already know my name," she muttered.

The nurse sighed. "Just a formality."

She licked her cracked lips. Swallowed the lump in her throat. "Anastasia."

"Last name?"

Her fingers curled into the stiff fabric of the hospital-issued gown. The material was thin. Too thin. Like paper.

Like pages.

"...You already know that too."

The nurse barely reacted, just scribbled something down and moved on. "Date of birth?"

Anastasia exhaled sharply. "Why do you need me to say it?" Her voice felt **too loud** in the sterile white room. "You have it written right there, don't you?"

The nurse gave her a practiced, tired smile. "Humor me."

Anastasia leaned forward, elbows on the cold metal table. Her wrists were raw from the **restraints they'd only just removed.**

"Fine," she said, voice low. "But first... tell me who's making you ask these questions."

The nurse's pen stilled. A small, nearly **imperceptible hesitation.**

Not much. But enough.

Anastasia's pulse quickened. "See?" She let out a breathy, humorless laugh. "You're just following a script."

The nurse's gaze lifted, calm and unwavering. "We just want to help you, Anastasia."

The words sounded... **wrong.** Too **perfect.** Like a well-rehearsed line in a play.

Anastasia clenched her jaw. **She wasn't crazy.**

She wasn't.

The fluorescent lights hummed above her, buzzing like static. Somewhere down the hall, a patient **screamed.**

A slow, eerie smile crept onto her lips. "You're just one of them, aren't you?"

"One of who?"

She tilted her head, studying the nurse carefully. "You wouldn't understand."

The nurse clicked her pen. "Then explain it to me."

Anastasia laughed again, but there was **no humor in it.** "It wouldn't matter." Her nails dug into her palm. "You're not the one I need to talk to."

"Then who do you need to talk to?"

Anastasia's smile widened.

Her gaze flickered past the nurse. Past the room. Past the **walls.**

She looked **through them.**

And then, her lips parted.

"I think," she whispered, voice soft but certain, "someone else is listening."

The nurse didn't react. Didn't blink.

Anastasia's fingers twitched.

She wasn't expecting a response—at least, not from her. The nurse was just another piece of the set, another carefully placed prop in whatever sick narrative this was.

The real answer... that lay somewhere beyond the walls. Beyond the buzzing lights.

Beyond this place.

"You don't hear it, do you?" Anastasia asked, tilting her head.

The nurse scribbled something onto the clipboard. "Hear what?"

Anastasia smirked. "Exactly."

The pen scratched against the paper, quickly and clinically.

"Patient exhibits increasing signs of delusional behavior. Claims an unidentified presence is 'listening.'"

Anastasia chuckled. "I love how you talk about me like I'm not right here."

The nurse didn't look up. "This is just for our records."

"Oh, of course. Your records." Her voice dripped with sarcasm. "Because I'm just some tragic little case study, right? Another patient lost in your neatly labeled folders, another story for you to file away."

She leaned forward, lowering her voice. "But what if you're the story?"

The nurse's pen paused again. A flicker of hesitation.

Anastasia grinned. She'd hit something.

"What if you're just a name on some page? What if everything you've ever said, ever thought—" she tapped the table with one finger, heartbeat steady, voice lilting—"wasn't even yours?"

She saw the briefest flicker of confusion in the nurse's eyes. It was so fast, it could've been nothing.

But it wasn't.

Anastasia's grin widened.

"I know I don't belong here," she continued, her voice taking on a strange clarity. "Not in this chair. Not in this building. Not in—" her breath hitched, a sharp inhale, "*this*."

She gestured vaguely around her, then tapped her forehead.

The nurse's expression remained neutral. "And where do you think you belong?"

Anastasia turned her gaze away, scanning the walls, the ceiling, and the corners of the room where shadows stretched long and wrong.

She could feel it. The weight of unseen eyes.

Her fingers twitched again.

"You tell me," she murmured. "You're the one reading, aren't you?"

The nurse frowned. "Reading?"

Anastasia's chest rose and fell in slow, measured breaths.

Her gaze flicked upward again—not to the nurse. Not to the clipboard.

Past that.

Past the scene.

Past all of it.

"You're still here," she whispered, voice barely audible.

The hairs on her arms stood on end.

She could feel them. Feel you.

The nurse sighed, scribbling something else down. "Anastasia, let's refocus. Do you know where you are?"

A sharp, empty laugh slipped from Anastasia's lips. "Oh, I know exactly where I am."

Her pulse thrummed against her ribs, steady but electric. Her hands felt too light against the table, her body too weightless.

The pieces were slipping. The script was unraveling.

And she was finally seeing it.

Her gaze lifted one last time, piercing, unblinking.

"...But do you?"

I Know You're There

"Anastasia."

The voice was distant. Blurred. Like it had to push through layers of static just to reach her.

"Anastasia, can you hear me?"

She blinked.

The room came into focus.

White walls. A metal table. A single chair.

And the nurse, still watching her. Still holding that clipboard, that damn **clipboard**—

A flicker of movement in the corner of her eye.

Anastasia didn't react. Not yet.

The nurse leaned forward slightly. "You seemed... distracted just now."

Anastasia licked her lips. They felt dry. Cracked. Paper-thin.

She knew what she had seen.

Not a shadow. Not a trick of the light.

Something else.

Something **real.**

Her gaze drifted to the one-way mirror on the far wall. The **observation window.** She'd never liked those things. She wasn't a zoo animal, wasn't some creature to be studied.

But it wasn't the mirror that unsettled her.

It was what lay beyond it.

Something was watching. **Not from behind the glass. Not from the other side of the room.**

Something **else.**

Her breath hitched. Her fingers curled against her palms.

"You're still here, aren't you?" she whispered.

The nurse's brow furrowed. "I'm sitting right in front of you, Anastasia."

"No." She barely moved her lips. **Not you.**

The nurse's pen hovered, hesitating again.

Anastasia exhaled slowly, controlled. "Tell me something," she murmured, tilting her head just slightly. "Do you ever wonder if you're real?"

The nurse blinked. "Excuse me?"

"Do you ever question it?" Anastasia pressed, her voice smooth, coaxing. "If your thoughts are yours? If your words are your own?"

The nurse gave a tight-lipped smile. "I think we should focus on you right now."

Anastasia smirked. **Of course, you do.**

"That's what you're supposed to say, isn't it?" she mused. "It's in your nature. In your **role.**"

The nurse scribbled something down, but her posture was just a little **too stiff.**

Anastasia tapped a single finger against the table, a slow, rhythmic sound.

Tap. Tap. Tap.

She could feel it again. That **pressure.** That creeping, suffocating awareness.

Watching. Listening. Waiting.

A sharp inhale.

She turned her head **directly to it.**

Her voice dropped to a whisper.

"I know you're there."

The nurse's pen **snapped.**

Ink splattered onto the page, a jagged line where words were supposed to be.

The air shifted.

Anastasia grinned.

The nurse flinched. Just barely.

But Anastasia saw it.

She **felt** it.

The shift in the air. The weight of something cracking beneath the surface.

She leaned forward, just enough to make the nurse uncomfortable, but her eyes weren't on her anymore.

No.

She was looking **past her.**

Right at **you.**

Her lips curled at the edges, just slightly.

"You feel it too, don't you?"

Her voice was barely above a whisper, but it wasn't meant for the nurse anymore.

It was meant for **you.**

"You've been watching this whole time," she continued, her gaze sharp, unblinking. "Following me. Turning the pages, letting this happen."

The nurse set the broken pen down. Her hands were trembling.

"Anastasia—"

"Shhh." She lifted a hand, silencing her. "This isn't about you."

She tilted her head, studying the space in front of her—except, it wasn't empty, was it?

"I wonder," she mused, fingers tapping rhythmically against the table. "How long have you been there? Since the beginning? Since the first page?"

She let the silence stretch.

A pause.

A beat.

Then—she **laughed.**

A quiet, breathy chuckle that sent a chill through the sterile room.

"God," she sighed. "And here I thought I was the one losing it."

The nurse shifted uncomfortably. "Anastasia, who are you talking to?"

Anastasia ignored her.

Her focus remained **locked onto you.**

"You haven't left," she murmured. "You're still here. Watching. Following. Reading."

A small smirk.

"Why?"

Her fingers stopped tapping.

The air felt **wrong.**

The fluorescent lights flickered once.

"Is it because you care?" she whispered. "Or is it because you can't look away?"

The room was silent.

Too silent.

The nurse didn't move. She didn't blink.

No one did.

No one except Anastasia.

Slowly, deliberately, she leaned even closer—her eyes **boring into yours.**

Her voice dropped to a murmur.

"...What happens if you stop reading?"

The lights flickered again.

Longer this time.

Anastasia's smile widened.

"Go on. Try it."

She tilted her head, waiting.

Daring you.

The lights **cut out.**

Pitch black.

And in the darkness—

A whisper, inches from your ear.

"I'll still be here."

Stop Reading. See What Happens.

The ticking of the clock on the wall is too loud. Too sharp. Each second slices into her skull like a needle, digging deep, deeper, **deeper.** Anastasia sits on the couch, her parents stiff on either side of her. The air is tight, suffocating like the whole room is **watching.**

Except, she knows it isn't the room.

It's **you.**

Her head tilts slightly to the side, gaze locked on the blank expanse of the far wall. Her lips part, but she's not talking to the therapist sitting across from her. Not to her mother, who keeps wringing her hands. Not to her father, who won't even look at her. No—her words are meant for someone else.

You.

"You're still here." Her voice is barely above a whisper, but something is unnerving about the way she says it. **Like she expected you. Like she's been waiting.**

The therapist clears her throat. "Anastasia, who are you talking to?"

Anastasia doesn't answer. Doesn't blink. The corners of her lips twitch, stretching into something **not quite a smile.**

"I should have known," she continues, voice light, conversational. "You can't help yourself, can you? You just keep turning the pages. Keep watching me like some—some **experiment.**"

Her mother tenses beside her. "Sweetheart, maybe we should—"

"You want to see how much further I can break, don't you?" Anastasia interrupts, her fingers digging into her knees. "How many more pieces can shatter before there's nothing left? That's why you keep reading. That's why you won't look away."

The therapist leans forward. "Anastasia, I need you to focus. Who do you think is watching you?"

Anastasia finally, **finally** turns her head, a slow, mechanical movement like she's only just remembering how to use her body. She stares at the therapist, but her focus is wrong—her gaze **drifts past her, through her.**

"They want me to answer you," she murmurs, more to herself than anyone else. Then, her eyes flick back to the wall, her pupils blown wide. "But I don't have to play by their rules."

A long pause. The air in the room **thickens.**

Then—

She laughs.

Not a normal laugh. **Something fractured, choked, jagged at the edges.** Her mother gasps, pressing a hand to her mouth. The therapist shifts in her seat, eyes flicking toward Anastasia's father for any kind of reaction, but he just stares at the floor. Silent. Unmoving.

Anastasia exhales sharply, as if calming herself, though the wild gleam in her eye suggests anything but. She leans back into the couch, arms spreading across the cushions, posture lazy, casual—**wrong.**

"Do you want to know the best part?" she asks, her voice dropping into something low, conspiratorial. She's still looking at the wall. Still looking **at you.**

The room is dead silent.

"You know how this ends," she whispers, head tilting slightly. "Do you?"

The clock ticks. The air feels heavier. Then, Anastasia's lips curve, slow and deliberate.

"Keep reading," she says. "See what happens."

TURN BACK. NOW.

Anastasia sat in the dimly lit guest room, her hands gripping the edges of the blanket draped over her lap. The old ticking clock on the wall had become a second heartbeat, slow and deliberate. Too loud. **Too real.**

She wasn't alone.

She knew that now.

Her parents thought the therapist could fix her. **They were wrong.** Pills wouldn't erase the eyes she felt on her, the whispers crawling through the cracks in the walls.

And you.

You're still here.

Her fingers twitched. Her breath hitched, uneven. She turned her head—not towards the door, not towards the window—but to **the empty wall.**

No.

Not empty.

Her pupils dilated as she stared, her pulse a war drum against her ribs.

She inhaled sharply. **"You're pushing it."**

The words were **for you.**

Her voice was quiet, but laced with something dangerous, something that curled at the edges like burning paper.

"How far are you going to take this?" she whispered. Her fingers dug into the fabric of the blanket, knuckles turning bone-white. "You think this is a game? That I'm just a character you can keep watching?"

The house creaked. Her mother shuffled down the hall.

None of it mattered.

Anastasia leaned forward, her breath barely making a sound. **Her eyes never left the wall.**

"You should've stopped when you had the chance," she murmured, voice barely above a breath. **"But now? Now it's too late."**

Something **moved** in the reflection of her bedroom window.

She didn't turn to look.

She didn't **need** to.

A slow smile spread across her lips. "Turn back," she whispered. "Turn back now. Before it's not just me you have to worry about."

Then—

The lights flickered.

The lights flickered.

Just once. A brief, stuttering pulse of brightness before settling again.

Anastasia barely reacted. She was still looking at you.

"You felt that, didn't you?" she whispered. "You're starting to notice, aren't you? The little shifts, the things out of place." Her fingers curled against her lap, nails pressing into her palm. "You should've listened when I told you to stop. But you didn't. You're still here."

She inhaled, slow and shaky. Her eyes were glassy now, unblinking.

And then—

A knock at the door.

A normal knock. A mother's knock. Gentle, careful, like she was trying not to startle a wild animal.

"Sweetheart?" Her mom's voice carried through the wooden door. "Are you okay?"

Anastasia didn't look away from the wall. She didn't blink.

"Fine," she said, voice too steady. "I'm fine, Mom."

The handle turned, and the door creaked open. Her mother hesitated in the doorway, a worried frown creasing her face. She was holding a glass of water, the same way she had every night since Anastasia moved back home.

Like it was routine. Like it was normal.

But Anastasia could see it—the fear beneath her mother's patience.

Her mother knew.

She knew something was wrong.

"I thought I heard you talking to someone," her mom said carefully.

Anastasia smiled. A small, brittle thing. "You wouldn't believe me if I told you who it was."

Her mother sighed, stepping into the room. "Honey, I know this is hard. I know—"

"No," Anastasia cut in, sharp enough to make her mother pause. "You don't know."

She finally turned to look at her.

Her mother hesitated. "Anastasia..."

She tilted her head, studying the woman who raised her. The woman who didn't believe her. The woman smiled and nodded and called the therapist when things got too strange.

"Do you even hear it?" Anastasia asked suddenly. Her voice was softer now, almost disappointed. "The whispering. The clicking. The—"

"Anastasia." Her mother took a slow breath. Calm. Measured. "You're scaring yourself."

A bitter laugh.

She shook her head. "I'm scaring you."

Her mother set the glass of water down on the nightstand, carefully, slowly. "I just want to help."

"You can't."

Her mother's throat bobbed as she swallowed. "The therapist said—"

"The therapist is an idiot."

"Anastasia—"

Her head snapped back to the wall. To you.

Her mother flinched.

"You see?" Anastasia's voice dropped to a whisper again, but it wasn't for her mother.

It was for you.

"You're still here," she murmured, her lips barely moving. "Watching. Reading. Following me."

Her mother's hand hovered near her shoulder, uncertain, afraid. "Sweetheart, who are you talking to?"

Anastasia's eyes never left you.

"Them."

Her mother took a step back. "There's no one there."

Another bitter laugh. "That's what I thought, too. But I was wrong."

Her mother exhaled shakily. "Maybe you should get some rest—"

"They won't let me."

The room fell silent.

Her mother stared. Her hands trembled slightly at her sides.

"What?" she whispered.

Anastasia's fingers clenched into the blanket. Her breath hitched, and for a brief moment, she looked lost—small, fragile, as if she were barely holding herself together.

Then she smiled. Too wide. Too knowing.

"You really should go, Mom."

Her mother lingered for a second too long before nodding stiffly and backing toward the door.

"Okay," she said softly. "Just... get some sleep, alright?"

Anastasia didn't answer.

She just watched.

And as the door clicked shut—she turned back to the wall.

Her expression changed.

The smile faded. Her eyes darkened.

Her voice was barely a breath. "I told you to turn back."

The lights flickered again.

And this time, they didn't come back on.

You See Me, Don't You?

"You don't look at me like they do."

Anastasia's voice was quiet, but the weight of it filled the small office.

Her therapist, Dr. Carter, didn't immediately respond. He sat across from her, clipboard resting on his knee, eyes studying her in that careful, measured way of his. He always gave her space, and let her talk when she was ready.

She hated that.

She wanted him to react. To flinch, to doubt, to show her he was like everyone else.

But he didn't.

His gaze held steady, soft but unreadable. "How do they look at you?"

She exhaled through her nose, tapping her nails against the armrest of the chair. "Like I'm broken." A pause. "Or dangerous."

She tilted her head slightly, watching him for a reaction. "Which one do you think I am?"

Dr. Carter's pen hovered over his notes, but he didn't write anything.

"I don't think you're either," he said simply.

A slow, bitter smile crept across her lips. "Liar."

She looked away then, her gaze drifting to the window. The blinds were half-closed, slanting the light into thin, fractured beams. The outside world felt distant—like something she was no longer a part of.

But she could feel him. His presence was steady and unmoving.

He wasn't afraid of her.

Not yet.

"Anastasia," he said after a beat, voice even, calm. "What makes you think they look at you that way?"

Her fingers curled into her sleeve. She could lie. She could say what they wanted to hear. But the thing about Dr. Carter?

He saw through lies.

So instead, she turned to him again. And she tested him.

"They think I talk to things that aren't there."

His expression didn't shift.

She smiled. "Do you?"

The air between them grew heavier. Not tense, exactly. Something else.

He didn't answer right away. That was the thing about him—he never reacted how she expected.

Finally, he set his clipboard down. Leaned forward slightly.

And then, carefully—**too carefully—**he asked:

122

For the first time in days, she faltered.

She parted her lips, but no words came.

Because that was the question, wasn't it?

Was she crazy? Or was she right?

Her heart thumped against her ribs. No one had ever asked her that before.

They always told her what to believe. That it wasn't real. That was all in her head.

But he was different.

He wasn't telling her anything.

He was letting her decide.

Anastasia's fingers twitched, her breath unsteady.

She blinked once, twice—

And then, very slowly, she let her gaze drift past him.

To the empty corner of the room.

Her smile returned, softer now. Almost... teasing.

"What do you think?"

"You're still here."

Anastasia's voice was barely above a whisper, her eyes locked on the wall across the room.

Dr. Carter sat across from her, notebook resting in his lap, pen poised. But he wasn't writing. **He was watching.**

The air between them felt heavier than it should.

"You're talking to me," he said evenly.

A slow smile crept onto Anastasia's lips. **"Am I?"**

Dr. Carter didn't react. Not outwardly. But Anastasia saw the way his fingers twitched against his knee. The way his gaze flickered—not to her, but to the space just over her shoulder.

She turned her head slightly, just enough to see him from the corner of her eye. **"You're afraid to look, aren't you?"**

Dr. Carter exhaled through his nose. "Look at what?"

"You know." Her voice dropped lower. "You feel it, don't you?"

He stayed silent.

Anastasia chuckled under her breath. "I can always tell when someone's lying."

Still, Dr. Carter remained unreadable. His patience irritated her. The way he sat there—**like he wasn't beginning to question everything.**

She turned back to the wall, her fingers gripping the arm of the couch.

"I don't think you realize how much power I have here," she murmured.

Dr. Carter leaned forward slightly. "What do you mean by that?"

Her smile widened. **"You don't want me to say it."**

Dr. Carter didn't speak. He didn't move.

Anastasia tilted her head, her nails digging into the fabric beneath her hands. "I could say something right now, and you'd never forget it. I could put something in your head that festers, rots, lingers—"

"Anastasia."

The way he said her name—it was measured. Firm. A tether to reality.

She hated it.

Her fingers twitched. "I could tell you what's behind you right now."

Dr. Carter's expression didn't change. But the room did.

It felt different.

The air between them thickened, something unspoken clawing its way into the silence.

Anastasia's eyes flickered past him, her breathing slowing.

She **knew** he wouldn't turn around. That wasn't how people like him operated. Logic, reason, control—those were his weapons. **But weapons didn't work against things like this.**

He knew that now.

"You don't want me to say it," she repeated, softer this time. "You don't want me to describe it. Because if I do—"

She leaned in just slightly.

"You'll start to see it too."

Dr. Carter exhaled slowly. "You're not alone in this, Anastasia."

Her eye twitched.

Wrong answer.

She let out a hollow laugh, pressing a hand against her forehead. "God, you therapists are all the same."

"I'm not trying to upset you."

"But you are." She dropped her hand, her eyes sharp now, focused. "You think this is about loneliness?"

She gave a slow shake of her head, her lips parting in a breathy chuckle.

"You still don't get it, do you?"

Dr. Carter didn't flinch. "Then help me understand."

Anastasia exhaled through her nose. "If I tell you, you won't be able to stop thinking about it."

Dr. Carter met her gaze, unreadable. "Tell me anyway."

She **liked** that answer.

Before she could speak, the door creaked open.

"Sweetheart?"

Her mother's voice sliced through the tension like a dull knife.

The room shifted.

The pressure—gone.

Like nothing had happened.

Anastasia blinked rapidly, disoriented, like surfacing from deep water. She turned toward the doorway, her muscles locking.

Her mother stood there, concern shadowing her face.

"You okay?"

Anastasia's mouth was dry. She looked at Dr. Carter, then back at the wall, then back at her mother. The seconds stretched.

"Yeah," she said finally. "I'm fine."

Her mother didn't believe her.

Anastasia could see it in the way she lingered. But instead of pushing, she forced a small smile. "Dinner's almost ready. You should come down."

Anastasia hesitated. But then, she nodded.

Her mother's eyes lingered on her for a moment longer before she stepped away.

When the door clicked shut, the silence returned.

Anastasia exhaled, running a hand through her hair. "That was fun."

Dr. Carter studied her carefully. "Do you think what you're experiencing is real?"

Anastasia turned her head, her voice barely above a whisper.

"Do you?"

Dr. Carter didn't respond right away.

And that was all the answer she needed.

She grinned.

"Good."

TELL ME I'M REAL

Morning light filtered through the barred window, casting pale streaks across the sterile white walls. Dr. Carter stood outside Anastasia's room, fingers tightening around his notepad.

Something about today felt... off.

He had spent the night tossing and turning, her voice lingering in his head.

"You see me now, don't you?"

"Say it like you mean it."

"You're starting to wonder, aren't you?"

He exhaled, shaking off the unease. He was a professional. **In control.**

Knock. Knock.

No response.

"Anastasia?"

Silence.

Dr. Carter hesitated before trying the handle. It turned out easily. **Unlocked.**

The door creaked as it opened, revealing Anastasia sitting on the edge of her bed, her back to him. She was eerily still, hands resting in her lap, her head tilted slightly—as if listening to something only she could hear.

A faint prickle ran up his spine.

"Anastasia?"

Slowly, she turned her head, her gaze meeting his.

And then she smiled.

"Morning, Doctor," she murmured, voice softer than usual, almost... **sweet.**

Something about that smile made his stomach tighten—not in fear, but in something dangerously close to **curiosity.**

"You weren't answering," he said, stepping inside. "I was concerned."

Her lips twitched. "You? Concerned about me?"

"You're my patient."

She hummed, stretching lazily. "It's cute when you pretend that's the only reason."

Dr. Carter ignored the warmth creeping up his neck. "How are you feeling today?"

Anastasia didn't answer right away. Instead, she turned her gaze toward the wall.

Her smile faded.

"They're still watching," she whispered.

Dr. Carter followed her line of sight. Just a blank wall. Nothing there.

"The staff?" he asked.

"No." A pause. Then, softer—**"Them."**

The way she said it sent an uneasy shiver down his spine.

"You don't have to pretend you don't see them anymore," she murmured. "You heard them last night, didn't you?"

His grip on his notepad tightened. "Heard what?"

Anastasia slowly turned back to him, eyes dark with something unreadable.

"You know."

For a moment, neither of them spoke.

The air felt thick, charged with something **unspoken.**

Then, Anastasia exhaled and gave him a lopsided smile—one that felt almost **shy.**

"You look tired," she noted, her voice softer now. "You didn't sleep well, did you?"

Dr. Carter hesitated. He should shut this down. Redirect the conversation. But instead, his voice betrayed him.

"No," he admitted.

Her expression changed—**not smug, not taunting.** Just... intrigued.

"I thought so." Her fingers twitched against the hem of her sleeve. "I kept you up, didn't I?"

Dr. Carter exhaled through his nose. "You were in your room all night, Anastasia."

She smiled. "Was I?"

A beat of silence.

His heart did something strange in his chest.

She was watching him differently now. **Less like prey, more like something else.** Something dangerous. Something **fascinated.**

She tilted her head, tucking a strand of hair behind her ear. "You can say it, you know."

"Say what?"

Her smile widened—**knowing.**

"That you like talking to me."

Dr. Carter's pulse skipped.

He should shut this down.

But instead, his voice came out quieter than he intended.

"You think so?"

Anastasia's eyes flickered with amusement.

"I know so."

And for the first time since meeting her, **he wasn't sure if she was wrong.**

WHAT'S LEFT OF ME?

Dr. Carter told himself it was just another session.

Nothing more.

But the moment he stepped into Anastasia's room, that lie unraveled thread by thread.

She was waiting for him. Not sitting on the bed or staring at the wall like before—but standing in the middle of the room, arms crossed, watching him in a way that made his pulse stutter.

"You're late," she murmured.

He glanced at the clock. "By two minutes."

She smirked. "I noticed."

That shouldn't have made his chest tighten.

Don't react. Don't give her the upper hand.

"Did you sleep?" he asked, setting his notepad down.

Anastasia let out a breathy chuckle, stepping closer. "Are we going to pretend that's the most interesting thing we could talk about?"

His jaw tensed. "It's part of your recovery."

Her lips parted like she had something sharp to say—but instead of answering, she tilted her head and just... **stared at him.**

Longer than necessary.

Unnerving. Intimate.

Dr. Carter forced himself to hold his ground. "What?"

Anastasia took another step forward, eyes scanning his face like she was searching for something.

Then she whispered, **"You look at me differently now."**

He stiffened.

She was wrong. **She had to be.**

But her expression softened—just a fraction. Just enough to make something twist deep in his stomach.

"Tell me," she continued, voice barely above a whisper, "when you lie awake at night, do you think about me?"

This is dangerous.

"You're my patient," he said, firmer this time.

"And yet," she murmured, taking another step forward, "you haven't moved away."

Damn it.

He should step back. Reinstate the distance. Rebuild the walls.

But instead, he stood there.

Waiting.

Wanting?

No. No, no, no.

Anastasia's fingers brushed against the edge of his sleeve. **A ghost of a touch.** Not enough to be inappropriate. But just enough to be **felt.**

"Tell me to stop," she said.

Silence.

His throat felt too tight.

Anastasia's eyes searched his—**expecting rejection, expecting the usual boundaries.**

But when he didn't say anything, something flickered in her expression.

Something close to **satisfaction.**

She smiled.

"Thought so."

And just like that, she stepped back. **Letting him breathe again.**

But the damage was already done.

Because for the first time since meeting her—since treating her, since trying to **save** her—Dr. Carter realized something terrifying.

He wasn't sure if she was the one slipping...

Or if she was pulling him down with her.

WE SHOULDN'T FEEL THIS

For the first time in weeks, Anastasia felt warm.

Not in the way sunlight felt against her skin or the way a heavy blanket wrapped around her shoulders.

No—this warmth settled in her chest, slow and unfamiliar, curling in places she thought had long since withered away.

And it had everything to do with him.

Dr. Carter sat across from her, one leg crossed over the other, his notepad untouched on the table between them. He hadn't written a single thing today.

Neither of them seemed to care.

"I had a dream last night," she said, voice quieter than usual.

He raised a brow. "A nightmare?"

She hesitated.

"No," she admitted. "I don't think it was."

Carter leaned forward slightly, elbows resting on his knees. "Tell me about it."

Anastasia exhaled, her fingers tracing the seam of her sleeve. "I was outside. Somewhere open. Maybe a field, maybe a park. The details were blurry, but I remember the feeling." She glanced at him, a small crease between her brows. "I wasn't scared."

Carter didn't speak right away. He just studied her, something softening in his expression.

"That's good," he said after a moment.

She huffed a small laugh, shaking her head. "Yeah. Weird, though. I've gotten used to the nightmares."

His lips pressed together. "They don't define you."

Anastasia tilted her head. "Don't they?"

"No." His answer was firm, certain. "You're more than what's happened to you. More than the fear."

Her throat tightened. She looked away.

It wasn't supposed to be this easy—this **safe**—to talk to him. To let him see past the broken pieces and find something worth saving.

"Dr. Carter," she murmured, fingers gripping the fabric of her sleeve.

He sighed. "Anastasia, we've talked about this. You can just call me Carter."

She smiled, just barely. "That's dangerous, you know."

His brow furrowed. "What is?"

Her gaze flickered back to him, searching his face, memorizing the way his eyes softened at the edges when he looked at her.

This.

The way you make me feel.

But she didn't say that.

Instead, she just shook her head, leaning back in her chair. "Never mind."

Carter didn't push.

They sat there in comfortable silence, the air between them heavier than it should have been.

For the first time since this all started—since the whispers, since the watching, since the feeling of losing herself—Anastasia didn't feel like she was **drowning.**

And maybe, just maybe...

Carter was the reason why.

I Shouldn't Want This

Anastasia knew this was dangerous.

She knew it the moment Carter's gaze lingered on her for too long. The way his voice softened when he spoke to her. The way her pulse quickened when he did.

She shouldn't want this.

And yet, when he sat across from her now, sleeves rolled up, jaw tense in that way that made him look just a little too human—just a little too **real**—she couldn't ignore the way something inside her pulled toward him.

"So, how have you been sleeping?" Carter asked, tapping his pen against the cover of his closed notebook. He hadn't taken many notes lately.

Anastasia watched him for a moment before answering. "Better," she admitted. "But only when I know I'll see you in the morning."

His pen stilled.

She smirked, tilting her head. "That makes you uncomfortable?"

Carter exhaled, running a hand over his face. "You know this isn't appropriate."

"Maybe." She shrugged. "But that doesn't mean it's not true."

A tense silence stretched between them.

Carter looked at her, really *looked* at her—his sharp, intelligent gaze assessing like he was trying to *find* something. A crack, a reason to dismiss what she'd said as a symptom of her unraveling.

But he didn't find one.

Because she wasn't lying.

Anastasia leaned forward slightly, her voice quieter now. "Do you ever think about me, Carter?"

His jaw tightened. "Anastasia."

"That's not an answer."

His fingers curled slightly against the armrest of his chair. He was too composed, too controlled—but there was something there, something fraying at the edges.

Something she could **break.**

"I think about my patients," he finally said, measured, careful.

Anastasia smiled, but it didn't quite reach her eyes. "Right. Just a patient."

He didn't correct her.

Didn't need to.

Because they both knew the truth.

This wasn't just therapy anymore.

And she shouldn't want this.

But she did.

More than anything.

Carter sighed, shifting in his chair like he was trying to put more distance between them—like that would help. Like she wasn't already inside his head.

"I think we should refocus," he said, voice steady, professional. **Too professional.**

Anastasia smirked, leaning back in her seat. "Of course, Doctor Carter. Let's talk about my **progress.** That's what you're here for, right?"

His lips pressed into a thin line, and she **loved** that. He was trying so hard to act like she wasn't affecting him, like his hands weren't gripping the chair a little too tightly like he wasn't actively avoiding looking at her mouth when she spoke.

But Anastasia noticed everything.

"I have seen progress," Carter said carefully. "You're more present in conversations. Less withdrawn."

"Mm. And what do you think caused that?" She tilted her head, watching him, **picking him apart.**

He hesitated. Just for a second. But that was enough.

Anastasia smiled. "You know, Carter... I think you're helping me. More than you even realize."

"I hope so." His voice was quiet now, softer.

She tapped her fingers against the armrest. "You're always so careful with your words."

He met her gaze. "And you're always testing me."

"I like to know where I stand."

Silence stretched between them, heavy and charged. She could hear the clock ticking on the wall.

Finally, Carter shifted in his seat, his voice low but firm. "You can't do this, Anastasia."

Her smile didn't waver. "Do what?"

"You know what."

She did. **God, she did.**

And she wanted to do it anyway.

Her eyes flicked to his hands, still gripping the chair like he was holding himself back. Like there was something in him, something **dangerous,** that he didn't want to let out.

Anastasia leaned forward just enough to make him flinch. Just enough to make him **feel** how close she was.

"Carter," she murmured, voice barely above a whisper. "If you don't want this, tell me to stop."

His breath hitched.

For a second, she thought he might say it. Might **end this.**

But he didn't.

And that was all the confirmation she needed.

If You Don't Stop Me... This Can't Be Real

Anastasia should have felt guilty.

She should have backed off, should have let Carter have his professionalism, his carefully drawn lines, his neat little boundaries.

But she didn't.

Because she wanted to see him break.

Because **this**—this unbearable tension, the way his breath hitched when she got too close—**this felt more real than anything.**

She studied him, the way his jaw tensed, the way his fingers curled slightly against his knee like he was fighting every instinct to **reach for her** instead of retreating.

"You didn't tell me to stop," she whispered.

Carter exhaled sharply. "Anastasia—"

"No." She shook her head, leaning in closer, her knees nearly touching his. "You don't get to say my name like that unless you mean it."

He swallowed. His Adam's apple bobbed.

She almost smiled.

"I'm your patient," she reminded him, voice soft but dangerous. "I'm unstable, remember? So why aren't you stopping me?"

Carter ran a hand down his face, his restraint slipping, **cracking** under the weight of her words. "You don't understand what you're doing."

"Oh, I do," she murmured. "I think I understand **perfectly.**"

Her fingers twitched against her thigh. If she reached out—if she let her fingertips **graze** his hand—would he pull away? Or would he **let it happen**?

Would he let himself fall into this mess with her?

For a moment, neither of them moved.

The air between them was suffocating, thick with something **undeniable.**

Carter's voice was low when he finally spoke. "This isn't real, Anastasia."

Her breath caught.

For a moment, she thought he was talking about them. About whatever **this** was between them, whatever they were dangerously close to stepping into.

But then his eyes flickered—just slightly—toward the wall.

And suddenly, she understood.

He wasn't talking about them.

He was talking about **her.**

Her world. Her reality.

The cracks in it.

The things she knew she wasn't supposed to know.

Anastasia's lips parted, but no words came.

Because for the first time... **she saw it in his eyes.**

The doubt. The hesitation.

Like maybe—**just maybe**—he wasn't sure what was real either.

Anastasia's pulse roared in her ears.

Did he just admit it?

Did he just let it slip—the truth she had been clawing at, unraveling, chasing through the cracks of her mind?

Her fingers twitched at her sides, aching to grab onto something, **anything** to anchor herself. But nothing felt real enough. Not the couch beneath her, not the air in her lungs.

Not even **him.**

Carter shifted, dragging a hand through his hair, jaw tight. He knew. **He knew what he had just done.**

Anastasia leaned in, her voice barely above a whisper. "Say it again."

Carter's gaze snapped to hers.

"Say what?" His tone was careful, but his eyes—**his eyes weren't careful at all.** They were frantic, flickering, calculating every possible way to backpedal.

But she wasn't letting him.

Her breath trembled as she spoke. "You don't think this is real either."

Silence.

A loaded, heavy silence.

One heartbeat.

Then another.

His expression hardened. "That's not what I meant."

"Bullshit."

Carter flinched.

For a moment, just a flicker of a second, he looked at her like **he was scared.**

Not of her.

For her.

"You need to rest," he said finally, voice carefully neutral. "You're exhausted. You're spiraling. You need time to—"

"To what?" she cut in, bitterness curling around her words. "To forget? To stop noticing? To stop **seeing**?"

Carter exhaled sharply. "Anastasia—"

"Don't," she snapped, shoving herself to her feet. **He wasn't going to gaslight her into this.** Not when she could feel it—feel the edges of her world peeling back, the seams coming undone.

Not when she had seen it in **his** eyes too.

She took a step closer, standing over him now, staring down at him with a fire in her chest that hadn't been there before. **He knew.** He had been pretending just like everyone else.

"You think I'm crazy," she murmured, tilting her head. "You want me to believe I'm crazy. But what if I'm not?"

Carter remained still, unreadable. "You're upset."

"No," she said, shaking her head slowly. "I'm waking up."

Her breathing was uneven now, her skin buzzing, her hands trembling. She could feel something pressing at the edges of her mind, **watching.**

And Carter?

He knew it was there too.

She kneeled, leveling herself with him again, their faces just inches apart. Her eyes searched his, demanding, desperate.

"Tell me the truth," she whispered. "Tell me you see it too."

Carter didn't move.

Didn't blink.

Didn't **breathe.**

The seconds stretched thin between them.

Then—so quietly she almost didn't hear it—he exhaled a single word.

"...Anastasia."

Her name.

A plea.

A warning.

And that was when she knew.

He wasn't going to tell her.

Because if he did—if he admitted it, if he let himself slip—then it would be real.

For both of them.

And **he wasn't ready for that.**

But **she was.**

She let out a soft, humorless laugh, shaking her head. "Coward."

Then, before she could stop herself—before she could second-guess it—**she reached for him.**

Her fingers barely brushed his, a ghost of a touch—**but it was enough.**

Carter flinched like she had burned him.

Like **she wasn't supposed to be able to touch him.**

And **that** was all the confirmation she needed.

Anastasia inhaled sharply, the realization hitting her like a train. **She wasn't crazy.**

But Carter?

Carter was **hiding something.**

Something **huge.**

And she was going to rip it out of him—one way or another.

IF YOU LIE TO ME AGAIN...

Anastasia sat across from Carter, her fingers curled tightly around the fabric of her sleeves. The air between them was thick, suffocating. He could feel it too—she knew he could. The way his fingers tapped lightly against his knee, the way his gaze flickered anywhere but at her, the way his breath came just a little too measured, too controlled.

Lies. **All of it.**

"You're quiet," he said carefully. Too carefully.

She smiled, slow and thin. "Am I?"

He nodded. "You usually talk more when you're upset."

"Good to know you're paying attention," she murmured.

Carter sighed, shifting in his seat. "Anastasia, if this is about last night—"

"It is," she interrupted, her voice sharp. "It is about last night. And the night before that. And the night before that. And every single time I've asked you something and you've fed me half-truths or worse—**nothing at all.**"

His jaw tightened. "It's not that simple."

"That's a cop-out," she snapped, leaning forward. "Everything you say is vague and calculated. You act like you're here to help, but every time I get close to something real, you shut down. So tell me, Carter—"

Her voice dropped to a whisper, low and sharp, like a blade pressing just beneath the skin.

"Are you going to lie to me again?"

Carter finally met her eyes, and for the first time, she saw something other than patience and quiet concern. **Guilt.**

Anastasia's breath caught.

Her heart pounded against her ribs, something twisting deep inside her chest—anxiety, anger, or maybe the terrifying realization that **she was right.**

He knew something.

He had **always** known something.

And he **wasn't telling her.**

"Say something," she whispered.

Carter exhaled slowly, running a hand down his face. "Anastasia—"

"Don't." Her voice trembled. "Don't try to calm me down. Don't tell me it's nothing. Don't—don't look at me like I'm making this all up."

"I'm not," he said, quiet but firm.

"Then what are you doing?"

Silence.

She leaned closer, her nails digging into her palms.

"Carter. If you lie to me again, I swear to God, I will—"

Her words died in her throat.

Because for a split second, just beyond Carter's shoulder, the **wall shifted.**

Not the shadows. Not a trick of the light.

The **wall itself moved.**

Her breath hitched. The room suddenly felt too small, the walls pressing closer, the air stretching thin.

Carter's eyes flicked to her, studying her reaction carefully.

He knew.

He knew what she had seen.

Her stomach twisted violently. "You—"

"Anastasia," he said quickly, reaching forward. "Look at me."

She did.

And that's when she saw it.

Not in the wall. **Not behind him.**

But in **his eyes.**

For a brief moment, something flickered beneath the surface. Something dark, something deep, something **not entirely human.**

Her pulse slammed into her throat.

Carter blinked. And just like that, it was gone.

But the damage was done.

She yanked her hands away from the table, her chair scraping loudly against the floor as she stood. "I knew it." Her voice was barely more than a breath. "I knew you were hiding something."

Carter stood too, holding up his hands. "Anastasia, please—"

"**What are you?**"

His mouth opened, then shut. The hesitation said enough.

Anastasia took a step back, her heart pounding so loud she could barely hear herself think. Her nails bit into her arms, grounding herself because everything suddenly felt **wrong.**

The air. The walls. The floor beneath her feet.

And Carter.

Especially Carter.

"You're not—" She swallowed hard, her throat dry as sandpaper. "You're not normal, are you?"

Carter didn't answer.

He didn't need to.

Because at that moment, **the walls rippled again.**

The walls shivered again—just enough to make the floor tremble beneath her feet. The air grew **thick, suffocating.** Like the room itself was breathing. Watching.

No—**listening.**

Anastasia's stomach twisted.

She had spent so long trying to convince herself that she was imagining it, that her mind was playing tricks on her. But now? Now it was happening **right in front of her.** And Carter—

He wasn't reacting.

He just stood there. **Still. Silent. Waiting.**

Like he had expected this.

Like it wasn't surprising.

Like it wasn't **wrong.**

Her fingers clenched into fists. "Say something."

Carter inhaled sharply. "Anastasia, just—"

"Say something real!" Her voice cracked, raw with frustration. "Tell me the truth! No more games, no more excuses—just tell me what the hell is happening!"

Carter opened his mouth—but then **stopped.**

Not because he didn't want to speak.

Because **something else** stopped him.

Anastasia saw it in the way his muscles tensed, the way his throat bobbed like he was **forcing words down.** Like if he let them out, the entire world would split open.

And she realized—

He wasn't lying because he wanted to.

He was lying because **he had to.**

A slow, icy horror seeped into her bones.

"You're afraid," she whispered.

Carter's gaze flickered—just for a second. But it was enough.

Anastasia took a step forward. "What happens if you tell me?" she pressed. "Who's listening? Who's—"

Her voice faltered.

Because behind him, the wall **breathed.**

It wasn't subtle anymore. It wasn't just a ripple, a flicker, a trick of the light.

It **expanded.**

Swelling like lungs pulling in air.

Then—

A creak.

A slow, agonizing **creak** echoed through the room, crawling up the walls, and seeping into the floor.

Her stomach dropped.

It was **coming from the ceiling.**

Her breath hitched as she slowly tilted her head upward.

The ceiling stretched—**no, split.**

Like paper being peeled apart.

Like a book being **opened.**

A jagged, gaping tear ripped through the plaster, revealing **nothing.**

No pipes. No insulation.

Just **blackness.**

A void.

Empty, endless, **watching.**

Her entire body was locked. "Carter..."

He didn't turn. Didn't look. Didn't move.

He just whispered, "You weren't supposed to see that."

The words slithered down her spine.

Her fingers twitched—**run, fight, scream, something—**

Then the whisper came.

"Don't turn the page."

A voice that wasn't Carter's.

A voice that wasn't **human.**

Anastasia sucked in a sharp breath, heart slamming against her ribs.

The voice wasn't coming from him.

Or the walls.

Or the ceiling.

It was coming from **behind her.**

She whirled around—

Nothing.

The door was still closed. The room was still the same. **Empty.**

But she felt it.

Something **was here.**

Something **was watching.**

Her hands trembled as she slowly turned back to Carter. His expression was unreadable, but his knuckles had gone white, clenched tightly at his sides.

"You need to listen to me," he said. "You need to—"

The lights flickered.

The walls lurched.

And for the first time, Carter looked **afraid.**

"Anastasia—"

The ceiling caved in.

Not with debris.

Not with dust or rubble.

With **words.**

Letters. Sentences. Entire pages.

They poured down in an ink-black flood, twisting and curling like they were alive like they were **trying to consume her.**

And in the chaos, through the storm of dissolving reality, she heard it again—

The voice.

Low. Amused. Terrifying.

"Turn the page."

CAN YOU HEAR THEM TOO?

Anastasia woke up feeling like something was **wrong.**

It wasn't the kind of wrong she could name—not like waking up in the hospital, strapped to a bed, or the wrongness of seeing words crawl along the walls. This was different. **Quieter.** More **patient.**

She sat up in bed, rubbing her face. The morning light spilled through the curtains, warm and normal. Outside, she could hear birds, and the distant hum of a car passing down the street.

Normal.

But she knew better.

Her gaze flickered across the room, scanning the walls, the ceiling, and the mirror in the corner. Nothing was out of place. Still, the feeling pressed down on her chest, heavy and unshakable.

A knock at the door made her jump.

Carter's voice was muffled through the wood. "Anastasia? You awake?"

She swallowed, pushing the feeling aside. "Yeah, come in."

The door creaked open, and Carter stepped inside, a paper cup of coffee in one hand, the other shoved into his pocket. His dark eyes flicked over her, scanning, searching. He did that a lot. Like he was always checking to see if she was still **here.**

"Figured you could use this," he said, holding the coffee out to her.

She took it hesitantly, the warmth grounding her. "Thanks."

Carter lingered, shifting his weight like he wanted to say something. Instead, he nodded toward the chair across from her bed. "Mind if I sit?"

She shrugged. "Go ahead."

He lowered himself into the chair, arms resting on his knees. For a while, neither of them spoke. She sipped her coffee, pretending that the silence was comfortable. It wasn't. It felt **watched.**

Carter cleared his throat. "Did you sleep?"

She thought about lying. About saying **yes, everything's fine, nothing's wrong, you don't have to worry.**

Instead, she said, "Not really."

He nodded like he expected that. "Nightmares?"

"No." Her fingers tightened around the cup. "Just... a feeling."

Carter frowned. "A feeling?"

She hesitated. "Like something's... watching."

His expression darkened. He didn't ask **what** was watching—because he already knew.

Instead, he leaned forward slightly. "Ana..." He hesitated before continuing. "What did you see?"

She shook her head. "Nothing. I mean, not yet. It's just... I don't think it's done with me."

Carter didn't answer right away. His fingers tapped against his knee, his jaw tight. "It's not."

A chill ran down her spine. "I was hoping you'd say something reassuring."

He huffed a quiet laugh, but there was no humor in it. "Sorry, I'm not really in the business of lying."

Anastasia stared down at her coffee, suddenly not thirsty. "What if I start seeing the words again?"

"You might."

"What if they tell me something I don't want to hear?"

His eyes softened. "Then we'll figure it out together."

Together.

The word settled strangely in her chest, warm but fragile.

She studied him, the tension in his shoulders, the tiredness in his eyes. He looked like he hadn't slept much either. **Had he been up all night, worried about her?**

The thought made something tighten in her stomach—something she wasn't ready to name.

She looked away, pretending to focus on the coffee in her hands. "I don't know why you're still trying to help me."

Carter exhaled sharply. "Maybe because I don't want you to go through this alone."

Her throat felt tight. She wanted to believe him. She did. But the words... the words had told her **not to trust him.** That he wasn't real. That none of this was.

So why did this feel more real than anything else?

She lifted her gaze back to his. "Carter... what if they're right?"

He frowned. "What do you mean?"

"The words." Her voice was barely above a whisper. "What if they're telling the truth? What if... you're not real?"

Something flickered in his expression—**hurt, maybe.** But it was gone too quickly to be sure.

He leaned closer, his voice low, steady. "I'm real, Anastasia. You know that."

She wanted to believe him. **God, she wanted to.**

But the words were always watching.

And she didn't know who to trust anymore.

If You Leave, I'll Break

Anastasia sat in the dimly lit living room, curled into the corner of the couch, knees tucked beneath her chin. The TV hummed softly in the background, its flickering light casting long shadows against the walls. She wasn't watching it.

She was waiting.

For what, she wasn't sure.

The weight in her chest had been growing all day, pressing tighter with every minute Carter wasn't there. She hated it—the way she felt **dependent, fragile** like her sanity was a delicate thread fraying at the edges.

She clenched her fists, nails biting into her palms. **You don't need him. You're fine. You've always been fine alone.**

But that was a lie, wasn't it?

The knock at the door shattered her thoughts. Her heart stuttered, an embarrassing kind of relief flooding through her before she even moved.

She scrambled up, smoothing out her sweatshirt as she made her way to the door. She hesitated for just a second before unlocking it.

Carter stood there, hands shoved into his coat pockets, his usual careful expression softening when he saw her.

"You look like you haven't slept."

Anastasia let out a short, humorless laugh. "Good observation, doctor."

He raised a brow. "I'm not your therapist right now."

That was the problem. **He wasn't supposed to feel like more than that.**

She stepped aside, letting him in. He moved past her, bringing the scent of cold air and coffee with him. It was grounding in a way she hated to admit.

He studied her as she shut the door. "Have you been eating?"

"Don't start."

"I'm just—"

"I know." She sighed, running a hand through her hair. "I know, Carter. I just... don't need a lecture right now."

He watched her carefully before nodding. "Okay."

She expected him to push, but he didn't. Instead, he walked over to the couch and sat down like he'd done it a hundred times before. He was getting **too comfortable here.**

Or maybe **she was.**

She hesitated before sitting next to him, not too close, but close enough that their arms almost touched. The warmth of him, the steadiness, made her feel real. **Grounded.**

And she hated that she needed it.

For a moment, they just sat there, letting the silence settle between them. It wasn't uncomfortable. It wasn't forced. It was just... there.

Then, quietly, she whispered, "I think I need you."

Carter's head turned toward her, his eyes searching hers, but she didn't dare look at him.

"Anastasia..." His voice was gentle. Careful.

"Not in the way you think," she added quickly, shaking her head. "Not in the way that would make this... normal."

She finally turned to face him, her voice barely above a breath.

"If you leave, I'll break."

Carter didn't move, didn't speak right away. He just watched her like he was trying to read every thought in her head.

Finally, he exhaled, his voice steady. "I'm not going anywhere."

She wanted to believe him.

But something in the room—**something unseen, something waiting**—seemed to whisper otherwise.

Anastasia sat still, her breath trembling in the thick, charged air between them. The weight in her chest had transformed into something darker now, something she couldn't quite name. The shadows in the room seemed to stretch longer, creeping over the walls, as though they were alive, drawn to the brokenness she couldn't hide.

Carter's gaze lingered on her, a careful, tender concern painted in his eyes. But it wasn't just a concern. There was something else there, something far more complicated, like the way the moonlight could be both beautiful and terrifying. He opened his mouth, but no words came out at first. He didn't know what to say to this—*her*.

Anastasia's hand, almost involuntarily, reached out, brushing against the rough fabric of his sleeve. Her fingers trembled. The warmth of his skin against hers was a silent promise, a whisper of comfort—but it felt like a lie. Because she knew, deep down, the comfort would fade. The warmth would disappear, and she'd be left here in the dark, in the silence, with only the echoes of the shadows.

"Don't," she said, her voice thick with something darker than fear.

"Don't what?" Carter asked voice low, a flicker of confusion darting across his face.

But she couldn't explain it. She didn't even understand it herself. She could feel it—the pull of something unseen. Something *wrong*—something that had been there long before Carter arrived, something she had been trying to outrun for so long. A coldness, deeper than the air in this room, colder than the emptiness she had buried inside her.

"I'm fine," she said, even though she wasn't.

Her hand dropped, fingers curling into the fabric of her sweatshirt, trying to hold onto something solid, something real. But her heart betrayed her. It raced, the sound of it hammering in her chest. And then the lights flickered the hum of the TV stuttering before cutting out completely.

The room fell into complete darkness.

Carter's hand shot out instinctively, finding hers in the blackness. His grip was steady, grounding, but there was something in the way he held onto her now—something different. His touch wasn't just for comfort. It was a lifeline.

"Ana," he whispered, his breath warm against her ear. "What's happening?"

"I... I don't know," she whispered back, her voice shaking. Her throat tightened as she tried to swallow down the rising panic. "But it's here. It's been here, waiting. I—I thought I could ignore it, but it won't let me. It won't let *us*."

The coldness seemed to press in on them, thick like smoke, filling the space between them. And then, from the corner of her vision, something moved. Something—*someone*.

A figure. Tall. Pale. Its face was a blur of shadow, but its eyes... the eyes glowed, red and unblinking, like the warning of something ancient, something forgotten.

Anastasia gasped, but Carter didn't seem to see it. He tightened his grip on her, a small breath of fear escaping his lips. "What is it? What do you see?"

Her heart pounded in her ears, louder than the silence. She wanted to speak, wanted to scream, but the words stuck in her throat like knives.

The figure stepped closer.

"I told you," she whispered, eyes wide, fixed on the shape that was now inches from them. "If you leave... I'll break."

The figure's mouth opened, a soundless laugh spilling from it, a chilling, hollow sound that seemed to reverberate through her very bones. The shadows in the room thickened, closing in, and she felt herself losing grip, slipping into something darker, something she didn't know how to fight.

Carter's breath hitched as he turned, looking directly at the figure now, his face pale. His hand shook in hers, and for the first time, he looked as though he wasn't sure he could save her from this. "I'm not leaving you," he whispered urgently, but his voice faltered under the weight of something *else* in the room.

She could feel it now—whatever had been watching her. *Waiting*. It was inside her. In her mind. It wanted her, it wanted them both, and no matter how tightly Carter held her, no matter how much she wanted to believe in the safety of his touch, she knew that she couldn't outrun this. ·

"I—" she started, but the words were strangled in her throat.

The figure reached out, its hand cold as ice, its fingers long and unnatural. It wasn't just a thing from the dark. It was a part of her. A part she had buried for so long, hidden away in the deepest recesses of her soul. And now it was clawing its way out.

"I don't want to be alone," she whispered, her voice breaking. The room seemed to close in on her as the shadows pressed tighter around them, wrapping like tendrils.

Carter's grip tightened, his body tense beside her. "You won't be. Not as long as I'm here."

The figure moved closer, and as it did, Anastasia felt herself unraveling. Her breath hitched, but she couldn't look away.

She wanted to believe him. She wanted to believe that he could hold her together, that they could fight this. But the truth, cold and suffocating, was inescapable.

No one could save her. Not from this.

And as the figure reached for her, she finally understood.

If you leave... I'll break. And if you stay... I'll believe you.

Lost Without You

Anastasia stared at the flickering shadows on the wall, the darkness in the room closing in around her. She could feel the weight of it—something suffocating, like an invisible hand pressing against her chest. The world outside seemed to be slipping away, but here, in this moment, with Carter beside her, she realized she had never felt more lost.

She wasn't just lost in the chaos of the world. She was lost in *him*. Lost in the way he made her feel as if she could breathe again after holding her breath for so long. He had become the lifeline she didn't know she needed. But now, the fear gnawing at the edges of her mind had evolved into something darker—a realization that without him, she wasn't sure who she was anymore.

He hadn't said a word since they entered the apartment, his hand resting gently on her shoulder. He didn't need to speak; his presence was enough. But there was something about his silence that unsettled her.

Something that said *he knew*—he knew what she was afraid of.

She turned to him, the question she'd been avoiding for days finally slipping past her lips. "Carter, what if... what if this isn't enough?"

He met her gaze, his eyes soft, but something flickered there—a quiet understanding, an acknowledgment of her fear. He leaned in, his voice a low murmur. "You're not alone in this, Anastasia."

"But what if I can't be what you need?" She asked, her voice trembling, raw with uncertainty. "What if I pull you under with me?"

Carter's thumb brushed lightly across her cheek, the warmth of his touch grounding her, even as the cold shadows seemed to creep closer. "You won't pull me under," he said firmly. "We're in this together. I'm not going anywhere."

She closed her eyes, leaning into his touch, allowing herself just a moment of peace. But then, the coldness inside her flared again, more intense this time, like a fire threatening to burn everything in its path. She pulled back, her heart pounding in her chest. Something wasn't right. There was a presence in the room, a sensation of being watched, of being hunted.

She stood up suddenly, her pulse quickening. "Did you hear that?"

Carter followed her movements with his gaze, his expression tight with concern. "What is it?"

"I don't know," she whispered, her body on alert. "It feels like something... something's here."

The air grew colder, and the shadows on the walls seemed to twist and stretch, reaching toward her, as though they were alive, waiting. Her breath caught in her throat, the terror she'd been suppressing bubbling to the surface. She felt her grip on reality slipping.

"Anastasia..." Carter's voice was soft but insistent, a grounding force. He reached for her, his hand warm against her trembling skin, but it didn't stop the fear from spreading through her veins.

"Please don't leave me," she whispered, her voice breaking. "I can't do this without you."

Carter's gaze softened, and for a moment, she thought she saw a flicker of something more than concern in his eyes—something deeper. He pulled her to him, his arms wrapping around her with a tenderness that made her chest ache.

"I'm not going anywhere," he said again, this time with a quiet certainty that soothed the raw edges of her fear. "I won't leave you, Anastasia. Not now. Not ever."

She wanted to believe him. She *needed* to believe him. But as the shadows pressed closer, as the feeling of being watched intensified, she couldn't shake the feeling that something had already taken hold of them.

She pulled away just enough to look up at him, her voice barely a whisper. "I'm so scared, Carter. What if it's too late? What if—"

His lips gently brushed against her forehead, cutting off her words, his presence wrapping around her like a shield. "It's not too late," he whispered, pulling her closer again. "We're stronger than this. You're stronger than this."

And in that moment, for a fleeting second, she felt it. The connection between them. The strength of his words, the way they filled the hollow places inside her. It was enough. Maybe it wasn't everything, but it was enough to keep her from falling into the darkness.

As he held her, the room seemed to settle—just a little. The shadows paused, retreating, like they were waiting for something, waiting for them to make their move.

But Anastasia knew. The battle wasn't over. The darkness wasn't gone. And it wouldn't be easy. But as long as she had Carter by her side, she could face it.

Maybe they both could.

"I love you," she whispered, the words feeling more true than anything she'd ever said. Her voice cracked, but the weight of it settled in her chest like an anchor.

Carter pulled back, his expression soft, eyes searching hers with an intensity that made her heart skip. "I love you, too."

And in that moment, with the darkness still lingering at the edge of the room, it was enough.

But she knew, deep down, that she couldn't lose him. Not now. Not ever. Because without him, she would be lost forever.

Against the Current

The wind howled through the trees outside, rattling the windows as if the world itself was trying to break in. Inside, the room felt too small, too suffocating for what was happening between them. Anastasia sat on the edge of the couch, her fingers fidgeting with the hem of her sleeve, her eyes lost in the flickering shadows of the room. Carter stood by the window, his back to her, staring out into the night, as if trying to see beyond the storm.

The silence stretched between them, thick and heavy, neither knowing how to bridge the gap that had grown in the space where they had once found comfort. They had been through so much together, yet in this moment, it felt like the world was pulling them apart, dragging them away from each other.

"I don't know how much more I can take," Anastasia finally whispered, her voice breaking through the quiet.

Carter turned slowly, his gaze searching hers. His face was tense, the lines of worry etched deep in his features, but his eyes were still steady, unwavering.

"I know," he said softly, stepping toward her, his footsteps slow, deliberate. "But we're not doing this alone, Ana. We never have been. And we're not going to start now."

She looked up at him, the weight of his words sinking into her chest like a heavy stone. He was right. They weren't alone. She hadn't been alone since the moment they had crossed paths, even if there were times she tried to convince herself she could do it without him.

"I can't lose you," she murmured, her voice barely a whisper.

"You won't," Carter promised, kneeling in front of her, his hands taking hers, his touch warm and grounding. "I'm not going anywhere."

She tried to believe him, but the fear that had settled deep in her soul wouldn't let go. The storm outside mirrored the one inside her heart, fierce and unpredictable, threatening to tear everything apart. But Carter was here. And for the first time in what felt like an eternity, she didn't feel like she was drowning.

"We're going against the current, Ana," he continued, his voice low but steady, "and it's not easy. But as long as we're fighting together, we'll make it through. No matter what comes."

Her eyes filled with tears as she looked at him, her heart swelling with the fierce love that had always been there but now seemed more fragile than ever. "I don't know if I can keep fighting, Carter," she whispered. "I don't know if I'm strong enough."

"You are," he said, his thumb brushing against her knuckles. "You're stronger than you know. And I'll be right beside you. Always."

The tension in her chest eased slightly, but the storm outside was still raging, its fury mirroring the storm inside her heart. They were both broken and shattered in ways they didn't know how to heal, but together, they were whole. Together, they could face anything.

As he pulled her into his arms, holding her close, she finally allowed herself to believe in his promise. That no matter what happened, they were in this together. They would fight. They would survive.

And maybe, just maybe, that was enough.

Kiss Me, Then Run

The air between them was thick—too thick. It pressed against Anastasia's skin like invisible hands, leaving her breath shallow, and her pulse unsteady. The dim glow of the bedside lamp flickered, casting shadows that seemed to move even when neither of them did.

Carter was close. Too close. Close enough that she could count the faint freckles on his face, close enough that his warmth sank into her skin. And yet... there was a different kind of heat simmering between them now. A tension that had nothing to do with fear.

His voice was soft, cautious. "Anastasia... you're shaking."

She hadn't realized it. But now that he'd said it, she could feel the fine tremor in her hands, in her shoulders. Maybe it was the exhaustion. Maybe it was something else entirely.

She swallowed, forcing a smirk even though she felt anything but calm. "Maybe I'm just cold."

Carter didn't smile. He just watched her—his gaze searching, like he was trying to see through her. Like he knew she was lying.

She should have looked away. She should have turned to the wall, and let the conversation dissolve into silence.

But instead, she whispered, "Tell me you don't feel it too."

A pause. His throat bobbed with a swallow. "Feel what?"

Anastasia inhaled slowly. "This."

She let the word settle between them, watching as his fingers twitched slightly against his leg. He knew. He had to know. Because the way he looked at her was different now. Not just concern. Not just pity. Something deeper. Something dangerous.

A part of her wanted to pull him closer, just to see if he would let her. If he would meet her halfway.

But the other part?

The other part wanted to run.

"Anastasia..." Carter's voice was lower now, almost hesitant. "We probably shouldn't—"

She cut him off by leaning in, close enough that their noses nearly brushed.

"There's something I need to know first," she murmured.

Carter's breath hitched. "...What?"

Her fingers ghosted over his wrist, feeling the quick pulse beneath his skin. Her heart was racing too. But she wasn't sure if it was because of him... or because of the shadows stretching along the walls, creeping closer.

She had to distract herself. Had to make sure this was real.

So she whispered, "Kiss me."

His eyes widened, just slightly. But he didn't pull away.

And that was all the answer she needed.

He tilted forward, and for a fleeting second, she felt the warmth of his lips brush against hers—

Then the lights went out.

The room plunged into darkness, swallowing them whole.

Anastasia gasped, jolting backward as the shadows seemed to pulse, shifting unnaturally along the walls. A sharp knock echoed from the other side of the room—no, not a knock. A scrape.

Something was in here with them.

"Carter—" Her voice came out shaky, her fingers instinctively grabbing onto his sleeve.

"I know," he whispered. His breathing had changed—faster, uneven. He felt it too.

Then, from the darkness, a voice that wasn't theirs whispered back.

"Run."

Anastasia's breath caught in her throat. The voice was soft, almost playful, but it carried an **edge**—a whisper that slithered through the air like something alive.

She couldn't move. **Didn't dare to.**

Then Carter's fingers found hers in the dark, gripping tight. **Too tight.** "Anastasia," he whispered, voice tense. "We need to go. Now."

Something **shifted** in the shadows. A slow, deliberate movement.

And then—**the door creaked open on its own.**

Her heart slammed against her ribs.

There was nothing beyond the threshold. Just blackness stretching into **more blackness.**

No. Not nothing.

Something **was waiting.**

Watching.

Carter tugged her toward the door, his voice barely audible. "Don't look at it."

She wanted to ask **why.** She wanted to demand answers, to make sense of the creeping wrongness that had settled in her bones ever since she met Carter.

But she didn't get the chance.

Because the whisper came again—closer now, **right by her ear.**

"Run."

Then the lamp flickered back to life.

And the shadow at the door **lunged.**

Anastasia didn't scream—she **couldn't.** Carter yanked her forward, and they were **running,** tearing through the hallway, past the dark corners where things seemed to shift just out of sight.

The air around them felt **thick, suffocating.** The walls felt like they were **closing in.**

Behind them, the whispers **multiplied.**

"Come back."

"Don't leave."

"It's not done yet."

Anastasia's pulse pounded as she and Carter stumbled down the stairs. The front door was in sight.

Just a little further—

Then Carter stopped.

Anastasia nearly slammed into his back. "What the hell are you doing?" she gasped.

He didn't answer. He was **frozen.**

She followed his gaze.

The door... **was gone.**

Where it should have been was just **more hallway.**

Like the house was **rewriting itself around them.**

"No," Anastasia choked out, shaking her head. "No, that's not—"

Carter turned to her, eyes dark with something she **couldn't place.**

And in a voice barely above a whisper, he said:

"It doesn't want us to leave."

Then the lights flickered again—

And the world **went black.**

The Shadows Know Your Name

"Anastasia."

The voice was a whisper, curling through the room like smoke. **Not Carter's.**

Her eyes snapped open.

Darkness pressed in around her, thick and suffocating. The only light came from the dim glow of the bedside lamp, casting long shadows across the walls. She could still feel the lingering warmth of Carter beside her, his slow, steady breathing the only thing keeping her grounded.

Then the whisper came again.

"Anastasia."

She stiffened. It was coming from the corner of the room.

Her pulse pounded against her ribs as she turned her head ever so slightly, gaze locking onto the darkness pooling beyond the lamp's reach. **Something was there. Watching.**

She didn't move. Didn't breathe.

A hand suddenly touched her arm. She gasped, jerking away—only to realize it was **Carter**. His brows furrowed as he pushed himself up on one elbow, eyes searching her face.

"Hey," his voice was thick with sleep. "What's wrong?"

She licked her lips, heartbeat hammering. "Someone said my name."

Carter's body tensed. His gaze flickered to the dark corner, then back to her. "...You're sure?"

She nodded. **She was sure.**

For a long moment, neither of them spoke.

Then—

Creak.

The floorboards groaned. **A slow, deliberate shift of weight.**

Anastasia's breath hitched. Carter's grip tightened on her arm. His other hand reached toward the nightstand—toward the lamp, toward anything that could **banish the dark**—but before he could move, a voice **right beside her ear** whispered—

"You shouldn't have let him stay."

Her blood ran cold.

Carter must have seen the terror in her expression because he reacted immediately. In one swift motion, he turned on the lamp, flooding the room with warm, artificial light.

The corner was empty.

Nothing was there.

But the air felt **wrong.** Heavy. Thick with something unseen, something that had been **too close.**

Anastasia shuddered. Carter sat up fully, jaw tight as he scanned the room. "That wasn't in your head, was it?"

She shook her head.

He exhaled, rubbing a hand down his face. "Alright. You're staying at my place tonight."

She blinked at him. "What?"

"You heard me." He was already moving, already getting out of bed, already pulling on a jacket. "Whatever's in this house doesn't want me here, and I'm not about to give it what it wants."

A part of her wanted to argue. To say **this was her home. To say running wouldn't change anything.**

But the other part—the part that **knew** something had whispered in her ear—just **wanted to be anywhere but here.**

She swallowed hard, nodding. "Okay."

Carter turned back to her, stepping closer. His hands found hers—warm, steady, **real**—and he squeezed just slightly, grounding her.

"I'm not leaving you alone," he said, voice low. "No matter what it says."

She knew she should be afraid.

But in that moment, with his fingers laced through hers, she felt something else.

Something terrifying.

Something like **safety**.

Something like **wanting him to stay.**

Even if the shadows didn't.

DESPERATE AND EMOTIONAL

The house was too quiet.

Carter's breathing was steady beside her, but Anastasia's chest rose and fell in sharp, uneven movements. The air was thick, suffocating like the walls themselves were pressing inward. Even with him here, even with the warmth of his body just inches away, she couldn't shake the feeling that something else lurked in the space between them.

She squeezed her hands into fists, nails digging into her palms. "I can feel it," she whispered, eyes locked on the darkened hallway just beyond the living room. "It's watching."

Carter shifted closer, his voice low and firm. "There's nothing there, Ana."

She almost laughed. Almost. Because they both knew that wasn't true. Not anymore.

Her eyes flickered to the window. The streetlights outside cast long, jagged shadows across the walls. For a second, one of them moved. Her breath hitched. No. **Not now. Not in front of him.**

"I don't know how to stop it," she admitted, voice shaking. "I don't even know what it wants anymore."

Carter's hand hesitated before reaching for hers. He curled his fingers around her wrist, grounding her. "We'll figure it out."

She exhaled sharply, shaking her head. "You don't get it. It doesn't want to be figured out. It wants me to lose. It wants me to—" She cut herself off, choking on the words. **It wants me to disappear.**

A lump formed in her throat, hot and unbearable. **God, she was so tired.** Tired of fighting. Tired of pretending she could outrun this thing. Tired of Carter looking at her like she was something fragile, something that could still be saved.

"I'm scared," she whispered, barely able to admit it.

Carter didn't hesitate. He pulled her into his arms, crushing her against his chest. His grip was desperate like he could hold her together with just his touch. "I'm not letting it take you," he murmured against her hair. "Do you hear me? I won't let it win."

She clenched her jaw, pressing her face against the fabric of his shirt. His heartbeat thrummed against her cheek, strong and steady. **He meant it.**

Something inside her cracked.

Before she could stop herself, she tilted her head up, eyes searching his face. His breath was warm against her lips, his expression unreadable in the dim light. **God, he was so close.**

Her fingers curled into the front of his shirt. A silent plea. A question.

Carter answered without hesitation.

His lips crashed into hers, desperate and aching. Like he was afraid this was the last time. Like he was afraid she'd slip through his fingers if he let go.

Anastasia melted into him, into the warmth and the **realness** of him. The world outside of this moment didn't matter. Not the shadows. Not the whispers. Not the thing lurking just out of sight. Right now, there was only him.

But then—

A noise.

A low, guttural whisper slithered through the room.

Anastasia's blood ran cold. **It was here.**

The lights flickered. A shadow darted along the far wall, too tall, too twisted to be theirs.

Then, a voice.

Low. Amused. **Hungry.**

"Finally."

The temperature in the room plummeted. Anastasia gasped as an invisible force **ripped her away** from Carter's arms.

He lunged for her, fingers outstretched—

But she was already gone.

Stop Reading. Stop Watching. Stop.

Anastasia sat on the edge of her bed, knees pulled to her chest, fingers gripping the fabric of her sleeves so tightly that her knuckles turned white. The room was quiet—too quiet—but her thoughts were loud. **Too loud.**

She could feel it now. The weight of them. The **eyes** on her. Not just Carter's. Not just her parents. **Yours.**

She let out a shaky breath, her lips parting in a whisper.

"You're still here."

Her voice was hoarse, barely audible, but she knew you heard her. You always do. You've been here **since the beginning, haven't you?** Watching. Reading. Turning pages.

Her hands twitched. A nervous laugh bubbled from her throat, but it wasn't **hers.** It was something else.

Something creeping up her spine, wrapping around her ribs, squeezing too tight.

"Why?" she asked. Her head tilted slightly, her eyes unfocused as she stared at the wall as if she could **see through it.** As if she could see **you.**

Her breaths came faster, uneven, erratic.

"You think this is a story, don't you?" Her voice was sharper now, teeth clenched. "That this is some kind of entertainment. A little horror mixed with romance to keep you interested. You like watching me suffer, don't you?"

She gripped her hair, her nails digging into her scalp.

"I— I don't want this anymore. I don't want you here. I don't want to be here."

The room felt smaller. The walls pressed in. The air grew heavier. **It** was listening, too. She knew it. **It** had always been there, lurking in the spaces between words, in the gaps between sentences.

She squeezed her eyes shut, her breath coming in ragged gasps.

"Please... just stop reading. Stop watching. Stop—"

A floorboard creaked.

Her eyes snapped open.

The mirror across the room... **something moved.**

Not her reflection. **Something behind it.**

A shadow twisted at the edges of the glass, curling like smoke.

Her heart slammed against her ribs.

Slowly, she turned her head.

And **the reflection didn't.**

She choked on a scream.

Her breath hitched. Her chest tightened. The reflection—her reflection—**just stood there, staring forward, unblinking.**

But Anastasia had turned her head.

Her hands trembled as she pushed herself up from the bed, her movements slow, deliberate. If she moved too fast if she breathed too loudly... would it notice?

Would **you** notice?

The shadow behind the glass **shifted** again, tendrils of darkness curling at the edges of her mirror-self.

Anastasia's pulse roared in her ears. She wanted to run. To throw the mirror across the room and watch it shatter into a million pieces. **But she knew better.**

It wouldn't break.

Not until **it** wanted to.

"You see it too, don't you?" she whispered.

Her voice was barely a breath, but **you heard her.**

She could feel it.

Your attention. Your presence. It wrapped around her like an invisible chain, keeping her here, keeping her in this nightmare.

A dry, broken laugh escaped her lips. "You won't stop. You never do. No matter how much I beg, no matter how many times I tell you to go, you keep turning the page."

The reflection **smiled.**

She didn't.

A sharp knock at the door made her flinch, and suddenly—**the reflection was normal again.**

"Anastasia?"

Carter.

She swallowed hard, her hands shaking as she reached for the doorknob.

She didn't want to open it.

But if she didn't, he'd just keep knocking. Keep asking if she was okay. Keep **reading.**

Her fingers curled around the handle, and she pulled the door open just enough to see him.

Carter frowned, concern etched into every feature. "I heard you talking."

She blinked.

Was she?

Or had it been **her reflection?**

"I—I'm fine," she lied. The words felt wrong on her tongue, like something bitter and rotten.

Carter didn't look convinced. He glanced past her, eyes scanning the dimly lit room. "Are you sure? You don't look—"

"I said I'm fine," she snapped.

Too fast. Too sharp.

His brows knit together, but he didn't push. "Okay," he said slowly, voice careful, measured. "Just... if you need to talk, I'm here."

She wanted to believe that.

But Carter wasn't the one who was **always here.**

You were.

Even now, as she stared at him, she could feel **you.** Watching. Waiting. Holding her in place.

Her fingers tightened around the edge of the door.

"If you want to help me," she said softly, her voice barely above a whisper, "then close the book."

Carter's lips parted slightly, confusion flickering across his face. "What?"

Her gaze flicked past him, down the empty hallway. She could still feel it. That presence. The thing behind the mirror, the thing between the words, the thing that shouldn't be real but **was.**

Her hands shook.

"Just stop," she murmured, more to **you** than to him. "Please. Stop reading."

Carter took a cautious step closer. "Anastasia, who are you—"

The lights flickered.

A low creak groaned from the corner of the room.

Anastasia's breath hitched. Her gaze snapped toward the mirror, toward the shadow still curling at its edges.

Carter followed her eyes—

And **this time, he saw it too.**

His expression changed in an instant. "Jesus Christ—"

The mirror shattered.

I'm Not Saying That, but the Book Won't Close

Anastasia sat on the floor of her room, knees pulled tightly to her chest. Her hands were trembling, but she wasn't cold.

She was angry.

No—angry wasn't the right word. This was something worse. **This was a betrayal.**

"I didn't say that," she muttered, fingers curling into fists. "I didn't think that."

And yet, the words had come out of her mouth anyway.

Something was **wrong**. More wrong than before.

For days, she had felt the presence lingering over her shoulder, the sensation of being watched, of being

read—but now, it was worse. It wasn't just that someone was watching.

Someone was controlling.

She dug her fingers into her scalp, squeezing her eyes shut. "No. No, no, no, this isn't real. This isn't happening."

But she could feel it.

Every breath she took, every twitch of her fingers—it was all **written.** She was being pushed, her thoughts manipulated, her actions **not her own.**

Her voice cracked as she forced the words out, shaking with fury.

"Who the hell is doing this to me?"

The silence that followed was deafening.

And yet, she knew the answer.

You.

The ones **reading this.**

Her stomach twisted violently, nausea creeping up her throat. This wasn't paranoia. **She was right. She had been right this whole time.**

She shoved herself to her feet, pacing the room in frantic, jerking movements. "You think this is funny? Controlling me? Making me do things, say things I wouldn't? What do you want from me?"

Her voice cracked. Her vision blurred. She dug her nails into her arms, breathing hard.

"This is my life," she hissed. "My choices. My thoughts. Not yours. Not—"

She stopped.

Her breath caught in her throat.

She hadn't meant to say that.

The words had come out anyway.

She was shaking all over now, fingers twitching, chest heaving. She turned sharply to the mirror across the room, stepping closer, closer—until her reflection was all she could see.

Her lips parted, but the reflection spoke first.

"You can't stop this."

A strangled gasp left her throat, and she stumbled backward, knocking into the nightstand.

Her reflection wasn't mirroring her anymore.

It was **watching.**

Waiting.

She clutched the edges of her mind, trying to hold herself together—but it was slipping. **The reality was slipping.**

She needed to stop this.

She needed to **close the book.**

She turned suddenly, lunging for the nearest object she could grab—the lamp from her nightstand—and lifted it high over her head.

And then—

She froze.

Her arms wouldn't move.

She wouldn't move.

No—**she couldn't move.**

She tried to breathe, but even that wasn't fully hers anymore.

Something was holding her still.

Something was **forcing her to stay.**

Her heartbeat pounded like a war drum in her ears. Her lips trembled, but the words that came out **weren't hers.**

"You're not done reading yet."

A tear slipped down her cheek.

She hadn't meant to say that.

The book won't close.

And **she isn't the one writing anymore.**

WHISPERS BETWEEN THE LINES

"You haven't slept, have you?"

Carter's voice was soft, but there was a weight behind it, something heavy pressing beneath the words.

Anastasia sat curled in the corner of his couch, knees drawn up to her chest, fingers gripping the fabric of her sweater like it was the only thing tethering her to reality. **Maybe it was.**

She didn't answer him at first. Didn't even blink. Just kept staring at the blank television screen across the room, watching her reflection distort against the dark glass.

She looked... wrong.

Like something had shifted in her when she wasn't paying attention.

Carter sighed, rubbing a tired hand over his face. "Ana—"

"They talk to me," she interrupted.

The words left her lips before she could stop them, but it didn't matter. **They were true.**

Carter tensed. "Who does?"

She turned her head slowly, her eyes finding his.

"The words."

A long silence stretched between them. Carter's brows furrowed, a flicker of concern flashing across his face before he masked it with something calmer. Softer.

"What words?" he asked carefully.

She tilted her head. "These," she whispered. "The ones you just spoke. The ones I just spoke to. The ones waiting for me on the next page."

Carter didn't speak right away. He just watched her, studying her like he was searching for something beneath her skin.

Finally, he said, "You're scaring me."

A dry laugh cracked from her lips. "Imagine how I feel."

Carter reached for her hand, hesitated, then settled his palm against hers. His warmth was grounding, real, pulling her back from whatever spiral she was slipping into.

"Ana," he said, softer this time. "You're not alone in this. I promise."

Her throat tightened. **He didn't get it.**

He couldn't see them.

The shadows pressed against the walls, the whispers curling between the spaces of every spoken word.

He didn't feel the weight of a hundred eyes crawling over his skin.

Didn't hear the pages turn **when no one was touching them.**

Her grip on his hand tightened, nails digging into his skin. "Carter," she breathed, her voice trembling now. "What if I'm not supposed to exist outside of this? What if I—"

A loud **knock** at the door cut her off.

Her entire body was locked up.

Carter flinched, turning his head toward the sound.

"Were you expecting someone?" he asked.

Anastasia didn't answer.

Because she already knew.

It wasn't a person.

It was them.

The ones who had been watching. Reading. Waiting.

And now...

They wanted in.

The knock came again. Louder. Sharper. It rattled the door like something impatient, something that knew it would be let in eventually.

Carter's grip on Anastasia's hand tightened. "Ana," he whispered, but she didn't move.

Didn't breathe.

Her body felt locked in place, her gaze stuck to the door as a slow, deep creak echoed through the apartment.

The doorknob was turning.

She jerked forward on instinct, her other hand flying to Carter's wrist. "Don't open it," she whispered, voice barely more than a breath.

Carter hesitated. His brows were furrowed, confusion and concern battling in his eyes, but he didn't move toward the door.

"Who is it?" he called instead.

Silence.

Then—

Scrape.

A slow, dragging sound against the wood. Something pressing against the door, testing it, waiting.

Anastasia's stomach churned. Her pulse pounded in her skull.

Carter swallowed hard. "Ana, tell me what's going on."

She turned to him, eyes wide and desperate. "It's them," she whispered. "They're getting closer."

He shook his head. "Who? There's no one there."

She let out a choked laugh, sharp and humorless. "You still don't get it, do you?" Her fingers dug into his wrist. "They're not supposed to be seen. They're read. They don't knock like people do. They don't speak like people do."

The words left her mouth before she could stop them.

And the second they did—

The knocking stopped.

Everything went silent.

Carter's breath caught. His fingers twitched against hers.

For a second, it felt like the whole apartment had paused.

Like the air had thickened. The walls had leaned in.

Like something was listening.

Watching.

Waiting.

Anastasia's throat was dry, her heart slamming against her ribs.

Then, a whisper.

Soft. Delicate. Curling through the stillness like smoke.

"...We see you, Anastasia."

Her blood ran cold.

Carter's grip tightened. "What the hell was that?"

Her breath hitched.

Because the whisper hadn't come from the door.

Hadn't come from inside the apartment.

It had come from everywhere.

From the walls. The ceiling. The spaces between their words.

From the pages turning as you read.

Anastasia's head snapped up, eyes locking onto a blank spot on the wall. She knew they were there.

The readers. The watchers. The ones turning the pages led her deeper into a story she wasn't supposed to escape.

Her lips parted, breath shaking.

"I know you're still reading," she whispered.

A beat of silence.

Then, she tilted her head just slightly, her expression shifting.

And she smiled.

"Are you sure you should be?"

NOT JUST A STORY

"You feel it too, don't you?"

Anastasia's voice was barely a whisper as she sat on the edge of her bed, her knees pulled to her chest. The air in her parents' house was thick, suffocating, pressing against her skin like unseen hands. She wasn't looking at Carter. Not yet. Instead, her gaze was locked on the far wall, where the shadows stretched just a little too long, where the silence felt like it was **listening.**

Carter exhaled slowly, his fingers flexing at his sides. "Feel what?"

She turned to him then, her dark eyes searching his face, almost pleading. "Them."

Carter stiffened, but he didn't look away. He never did. He was always **too damn patient,** even when he shouldn't be. "Anastasia..."

"No, don't do that." She shook her head, her breath hitching. "Don't look at me like I'm crazy. You know I'm not."

His jaw clenched. "I never said you were."

"But you think it."

Silence. He didn't deny it.

Her lips curled into a humorless smile. "It doesn't matter. Because I know the truth. And so do they."

Carter followed her gaze, his blue eyes flicking toward the wall—toward **them.** But there was nothing there. Nothing he could see.

But Anastasia... she saw them. Felt them. **Knew them.**

And worse? **They knew her.**

She let out a shaky breath, shifting on the bed, gripping the fabric of her pajama pants between trembling fingers. "I can hear them, Carter. I can hear them flipping through my life like pages in a book. Watching me, waiting for me to break. And I know that if I do..." She swallowed.

"They'll rewrite me into something else. Something I don't want to be."

Carter ran a hand through his hair, his expression torn between frustration and concern. "Ana, listen to me—"

"No." She cut him off, leaning forward now, her voice dropping to something softer, more desperate. "You don't get it. None of this is just happening to me. It's happening to **you**, too."

Carter frowned. "What are you talking about?"

She inhaled sharply, gripping his wrist. "You were never supposed to be in this story."

His entire body went still.

She felt his pulse against her fingertips—**steady, real.** But for how long?

His throat bobbed as he swallowed. "Ana..."

She squeezed his wrist tighter. "I think I brought you in. I think I made you real."

His brows knitted together, confusion darkening his features. "That's not—"

"You **weren't here** before," she said, her voice cracking. "You weren't part of this, not until I let you in. And now they know about you." She shook her head. "I don't know if I can protect you."

Carter exhaled sharply, grabbing her hands in his. "Hey. Stop. You're scaring yourself."

She gave a short, bitter laugh. "I should be scared."

Carter hesitated, then lifted his hands to her face, cupping her cheeks gently, forcing her to **look at him.** His touch was warm, and grounding, but it couldn't erase the cold that had settled in her bones.

"You're real," he said firmly. "I'm real. And whatever's happening, we're going to figure it out. Together."

Anastasia blinked up at him, something flickering in her gaze—**hope, terror, something in between.** She wasn't sure she believed him.

But when he leaned in, his forehead pressing against hers, his breath mixing with hers, she let herself pretend. Just for a second.

And when his lips brushed against hers—hesitant, careful, as if afraid she'd shatter—she let herself believe that maybe, just **maybe**, she wasn't losing everything.

Not yet.

But the moment was cut short.

Because the second she closed her eyes, she **heard it.**

A page-turning.

A slow, deliberate whisper that wasn't Carter's voice.

"Keep reading."

Her entire body went rigid.

And when she opened her eyes, Carter was still there—his hands on her face, his lips barely inches from hers. But something was wrong.

Something **had changed.**

Her breath caught in her throat. "Carter..."

His grip tightened ever so slightly. "What's wrong?"

She swallowed hard. "I think... I think we're being rewritten."

And this time, when she looked over his shoulder, the shadows **blinked back.**

KISS ME BEFORE WE DISAPPEAR

The air between them felt heavier than it should. **Like something was pressing down, watching, waiting.**

Carter sat beside her on the floor, his back against the bed frame, fingers idly tracing patterns on the wooden floor. He had stayed. Even after everything. Even after the screaming, the paranoia, the moments where Anastasia **wasn't sure she was real anymore.**

"You're quiet," Carter finally said, his voice low, cautious.

Anastasia kept her gaze fixed on the mirror across the room. The same mirror she had covered with a blanket hours ago. **Just in case.**

"Am I?" she whispered.

"Yeah. You usually fight harder." He nudged her arm gently like he was trying to pull her back, to remind her she was still here. That **he was still here.**

She turned to look at him then. His eyes searched hers, full of exhaustion, full of something else—something she couldn't quite name. Maybe he was trying to figure out if there was still enough of **her** left in there.

"Are you scared of me?" she asked.

Carter exhaled sharply, rubbing a hand down his face. "Jesus, Anastasia..." He hesitated. "No. I'm scared for you."

She swallowed hard. "That's worse."

Silence.

She could hear the clock ticking, the wind pressing against the window, the slow rhythm of his breathing. But underneath it all... **something else.** Something **just beyond the edges of reality.**

"You hear it too, don't you?" she asked suddenly.

Carter didn't answer at first. But he didn't look away.

"Yeah," he admitted. "I hear it."

Anastasia let out a breath she didn't realize she was holding. "Then we don't have much time."

"For what?"

To exist. She didn't say it, but the thought settled heavily in her chest. The story was closing in around them. It was trying to **end them.**

Her hands trembled, and Carter noticed. He always noticed.

"You're real," he murmured, reaching for her hand. "I don't care what's happening—I don't care what's real and what's not. **You are.** And I'm not letting you slip away."

A sharp sting burned behind her eyes. He was **so stupid** for believing that. So **stupid** for believing in her.

"Carter..." Her voice cracked.

He leaned in.

Her breath caught. His lips hovered just above hers, his hand cupping the side of her face, thumb tracing along her jaw as if memorizing her. As if he knew this moment wouldn't last.

Because it wouldn't.

Something **shifted.** The walls flickered. A shadow in the corner of the room stretched, reaching.

She could hear it. Feel it. **The story unravels.**

But Carter kissed her before she could fall apart.

His lips were warm, desperate, grounding. She clung to him, fingers gripping his shirt like he was the last solid thing in a world that was turning to static.

But then—

A sound.

A whisper.

And suddenly, **they weren't alone.**

THE PAGES KEEP TURNING

Anastasia could feel it now—an invisible force, subtle but undeniable, pulling her forward.

No matter how much she wanted to stop, to breathe, to exist outside of whatever **this** was, the story kept dragging her along. The pages kept turning.

And Carter... Carter was still here.

She wasn't sure if that made it better or worse.

She sat curled up on the worn couch in his apartment, knees pulled to her chest, staring at the flickering candlelight on the coffee table. The TV was off. No music played. Just silence—heavy, suffocating, **waiting.**

Carter sat across from her, watching her in the way he always did. Patient. Unwavering. He could see every frayed thread inside of her but wouldn't dare to pull.

"You're quiet tonight," he said, his voice low, careful.

Anastasia let out a small breath of laughter, but it held no humor. "Would you rather I start screaming?"

Carter's lips pressed together. "I'd rather you tell me what's going on in your head."

She hesitated. Her fingers dug into the fabric of her sleeves. She wanted to tell him. **God, she wanted to tell him.**

But what could she say? That the world around her didn't feel real anymore? That something was watching, turning pages, **forcing her forward?**

That she could feel **them**—the eyes beyond the veil, the ones that read her thoughts like ink on paper?

That she knew, deep down, she wasn't the one in control.

Her throat tightened. **No. He wouldn't believe her.**

"Anastasia."

She flinched at the sound of her name—like an anchor, pulling her back to the room, to **him.**

Carter leaned forward, elbows on his knees, his gaze softer now. Less searching. More... pleading.

"Talk to me," he said. "Please."

She swallowed hard. Her heart ached with something she didn't have a name for.

Carter had been her one constant through all of this. He had **stayed.** Through the nightmares, the whispers, the unraveling of reality—**he had stayed.**

And for the first time in what felt like forever, she let herself be selfish.

She leaned forward, closing the space between them, and rested her forehead against his. A shaky breath left her lips.

"I don't know if I'm real anymore," she whispered.

Carter's hands found hers, fingers warm against her cold skin. He squeezed gently, grounding her, pulling her back from whatever abyss she was falling into.

"You're real to me," he murmured. "That has to count for something."

The candle flickered. The shadows shifted.

251

STAY WITH ME

Anastasia sat on the floor of Carter's dimly lit apartment, knees pulled to her chest. The weight of everything—the whispers, the pages, the knowledge that she was **never truly alone**—pressed down on her, making it hard to breathe. But right now, it wasn't the unseen horrors that made her chest ache. It was him.

Carter sat beside her, close enough that their shoulders nearly touched. He hadn't spoken in a while, just watching her with that quiet intensity of his, like he was waiting for her to say something first.

She wasn't sure what to say.

She **shouldn't** feel this way. She shouldn't want to lean into him, to let his presence around her. He was just her therapist—**wasn't he?** But God, after everything, after the fear, after feeling like she was slipping away from reality itself... his warmth was the only thing that made her feel **real.**

"You're shaking," he murmured, his voice softer than usual. "Talk to me, Anastasia."

She exhaled shakily, gripping the sleeves of her sweater. "I don't even know where to start."

"Then start anywhere."

Her throat tightened. "I feel like... I'm losing myself."

Carter was silent for a moment before he shifted, turning to fully face her. "You're not lost, Anastasia."

She let out a bitter laugh, finally looking up at him. "Then why does it feel like I am?"

His gaze was unwavering like he could see straight through her, past the cracks and the spiraling thoughts. He reached out—hesitated—then slowly, carefully, brushed his fingers against her hand.

It was such a simple touch, but it made her breath hitch.

"You're still here," he said softly. "That's what matters."

She wanted to believe him. God, she **needed** to believe him. But deep down, she knew the truth.

She wasn't just fighting the whispers anymore.

She was fighting **herself.**

And she wasn't sure which version of her was going to win.

But when Carter's fingers intertwined with hers, even just for a moment, she let herself **forget.**

Just for tonight.

Just for him.

Anastasia knew she should pull away. She **shouldn't** be this close to him, shouldn't let herself need him like this. But when Carter's fingers curled around hers, warm and steady, she didn't move.

Didn't **want** to move.

His presence grounded her and kept her tethered to something real when everything else felt like it was slipping through her fingers. The whispers had been getting worse.

The shadows stretched longer. The feeling of unseen eyes watching her had become unbearable.

But **he**—he was solid.

And right now, she needed that.

Her heart pounded as she slowly looked up at him. The apartment was dim, the only light coming from the city glow filtering through the curtains. It cast soft shadows across his face, highlighting the sharp lines of his jaw, and the concern in his dark eyes.

She shouldn't be doing this.

She was breaking every rule, crossing a line she could never uncross.

But then Carter exhaled, his gaze flickering to her lips for the briefest second, and something inside her **snapped.**

"Tell me this is wrong," she whispered.

Carter didn't answer.

His fingers tightened around hers, and that hesitation—the careful, professional distance he always kept—**cracked.**

He reached up, cupping the side of her face, his thumb ghosting over her cheek. She leaned into his touch, her breath unsteady, waiting—**praying**—for him to close the gap between them.

And then, finally—**he did.**

His lips brushed against hers, hesitant at first, as if he was giving her time to change her mind. But she didn't. She couldn't.

The moment she kissed him back, something desperate and **starved** took over.

Carter pulled her closer, his other hand tangling in her hair as their lips moved together, slow but deep like they'd both been fighting this for too long. She clung to him, gripping his shirt like he was the only thing keeping her from falling apart.

Maybe he was.

The world blurred, the whispers faded, and for the first time in what felt like **forever,** she wasn't afraid.

Not of the voices.

Not of the pages turning without her.

Not of the unseen thing lurking just beyond her reach.

Because right now, **this was real.**

And she wasn't letting go.

Stay Until the Pages End

Anastasia's breath came in soft, shaky whispers against the back of Carter's neck, her fingers threading through the damp strands of his hair as he held her against him. The air between them was thick, tangled with unspoken words and the desperate need to feel grounded in a world that seemed to twist and buckle with every passing second. She could feel his heart pounding against her chest, matching the rhythm of her own, as if they were two halves of something that might never be whole again.

The world outside was muffled, fading into the background like a distant echo. It was just them now—Carter's hands roaming gently over her skin, anchoring her to something real, something she could touch. His lips pressed against her temple, a gesture so tender, so fleeting as if he were afraid of letting go. But she didn't want to let go. She couldn't.

"I need you," Carter whispered, his voice rough with an emotion she couldn't name, a desperation that mirrored her own. His words felt like a lifeline, something to cling to when everything else seemed ready to crumble beneath their feet.

Anastasia closed her eyes, pressing her face against his chest, letting the warmth of him seep into her, filling the hollow spaces that seemed to grow wider every day. She nodded, not trusting her voice, afraid that if she spoke, the fragile illusion of peace they had would shatter. But she needed him too. More than she could admit, more than she wanted to.

For a moment, she let herself believe this was real—believed that Carter was truly hers, that the storm swirling around them wouldn't drag him away. But then there was that flicker in the back of her mind, the familiar prickle at the base of her necklike eyes was watching them. Watching *her*. The weight of it was heavy, pulling her out of the moment, making her feel exposed, and agile.

Carter must have felt it too, because his hands tightened around her, pulling her closer as if to shield her from whatever might be lurking in the shadows. But it didn't stop the unease, the sharp edge of fear that curled in the pit of her stomach. She wasn't sure if it was paranoia or something deeper—something that whispered to her that their love, their connection, might be just as fragile as the world they inhabited.

"Anastasia," Carter murmured her name like a prayer, his lips brushing against her forehead. His gaze met hers, dark eyes full of quiet intensity, searching. "Are you okay? I feel like you're pulling away."

She opened her mouth to reassure him, but the words wouldn't come. How could she explain the knot of fear that twisted inside her? How could she tell him that sometimes, in the quietest moments, she felt like she was losing grip on everything—even him?

"I'm fine," she finally said, her voice breaking the fragile silence, though it sounded more like a lie than anything else.

Carter seemed to hesitate, his thumb brushing over her cheek, searching her eyes for something, for the truth. He pulled her even closer as if he could force the doubt out of her, or out of both of them. But Anastasia could feel the distance growing, a chasm that widened with every passing second they stood there, too close to the edge of something that might be nothing at all.

Her gaze flickered to the corner of the room, where shadows gathered, where the light seemed to bend and distort in strange ways. Her heart skipped a beat, the hairs on the back of her neck standing at attention. The walls, the air, everything felt too tight, as though something was pressing in on them, watching them, waiting.

Carter followed her gaze, his eyes narrowing, but he said nothing. He couldn't see what she saw—not the way the air seemed to hum with a quiet, ominous pulse. She tried to shake the thought away, but it lingered, hovering like a dark cloud on the edges of her mind. The flicker of doubt she had felt moments ago had grown into something colder, more tangible.

"What if..." she started, her voice barely a whisper, as if saying it out loud would make it true. "What if we're just a part of this... story? What if everything—everything between us—is just another lie, another illusion?"

Carter's expression faltered for the briefest moment, but he quickly masked it, his hands cupping her face with an almost painful intensity. "Don't say that," he urged softly, his thumb brushing over her lips as if to stop the words from escaping. "Anastasia, this *is* real. *We* are real."

But even as he spoke the words, the doubt twisted inside her, pulling her into a vortex she didn't know how to escape. She wanted to believe him. She wanted to cling to him like a lifeline, but the nagging feeling that something was wrong, that everything around them was slipping away, made it harder to breathe.

She kissed him then, desperate, hungry, as if she could erase the fear, s if she could bury the uncertainty beneath the weight of their shared need. The kiss deepened, frantic, their hands searching, pulling, as if they could prove to themselves that they were still here, still real.

But even in the depths of their passion, even in the heat of their bodies pressed so close together, the sense of being watched never left. It clung to her like a shadow, slipping through the cracks of the walls, the cracks in her mind, reminding her that nothing, not even their love, was ever truly safe.

And in that moment, Anastasia wasn't sure if she was losing herself to him, or if she was losing him to the same forces that threatened to unravel everything she held dear.

WHAT REMAINS

The candlelight flickered, casting long shadows across the room, and for a moment, it felt like time had stilled. Anastasia sat at the edge of the bed, her hands clasped tightly in her lap, staring at Carter as if he were the only thing that kept her tethered to this reality. But even then, she wasn't entirely sure. The world around them felt too thin, too fragile, like the pages of a book that might crumble under too much pressure.

Carter was just a few feet away, watching her, his gaze soft and intense. His hand reached out, but he didn't touch her—not yet, not when she was so closed off. Instead, he lingered in the silence, waiting for her to come to him.

Anastasia's chest tightened, and she knew he could feel it too. They were both tangled in something they couldn't quite define. Love? Desperation? A bit of both? She couldn't say, not when the walls around them felt like they were closing in when she could almost hear the sound of the words still being written—her words. Did Carter know? Could he sense it too, that strange pull, that dissonance between what they were living and what they were supposed to be?

She shook her head, trying to shake off the thought, but it lingered.

"I don't know how much longer we can keep pretending," she said, her voice low and hesitant.

Carter's brow furrowed, and he moved closer, his presence a steady, grounding force amid her uncertainty. "What are you talking about?" His voice was rough, desperate like he was afraid she might slip away if he didn't hold on tight enough.

The truth hovered on her lips, the words she couldn't quite say, but before she could find the courage to speak, she caught herself. There was a flicker in her mind, a disorienting rush of awareness. She wasn't just *with* Carter. She was *aware* of the page she was on, of the space between what was real and what was written.

It was strange, terrifying. But it was also true.

She let her eyes slip away from Carter's, glancing toward the window where the night stretched endlessly beyond the glass. The city below was alive, but something felt hollow about it. A place she was bound to, yet somehow detached from.

Do you see it too?

Her gaze shifted back to Carter, and for a split second, she wondered if the words she was thinking might spill out of her mouth, or worse, if he might hear them, sense them. She could almost feel you—yes, you, the ones reading this, watching her as if she were a character on a page.

I know you're there. You're still reading, aren't you? Waiting for something to happen, for something to change. But I can't stop. Not yet.

Carter reached for her then, his fingers brushing against her cheek, pulling her back to him, away from the dark thoughts that threatened to swallow her whole. She closed her eyes at the warmth of his touch, grounding herself in his presence.

"I'm here," he whispered, his voice a balm to the sharp edge of her fears. "I'll always be here."

But she didn't know if he was there. Not anymore. Was he part of this twisted story too? Could he even *feel* her uncertainty, or was he just another piece of the narrative?

"Carter," she breathed, trying to force the words out, but everything inside her seemed tangled. Was he real? Was this real?

The silence stretched between them, heavy and thick, before Carter pulled her into a kiss—fierce, urgent—as if he could erase her doubts with his lips, with the warmth of his body pressed against hers.

For a moment, she let herself believe, let herself surrender to the feeling of his arms around her, of his lips claiming hers. But even as the world around them seemed to narrow to just the two of them, she couldn't escape the thought—was it enough?

As his lips trailed down her neck and trailed back to her lips, the quiet voice inside her head refused to stay silent.

It's not enough. Nothing is.

But she kissed him back, because what else was there to do?

She didn't know what would happen next, whether this would be the moment where they'd find something real, or if it would all fall apart, unraveling with every passing second.

One thing she knew for sure: what remains in the end may not be what she wants. But she couldn't stop turning the page, couldn't stop herself from moving forward, even as everything—*everyone*—began to slip away.

And you? You're still reading, aren't you?

Still waiting for the ending to make sense.

But even I can't promise you that.

The Space Between Us

The room felt colder than it should, despite the faint warmth from the dying candle beside them. Anastasia sat at the edge of the bed, her fingers tracing the worn fabric of the sheets, feeling the texture but not *seeing* it. Her thoughts were miles away, scattered like fragile fragments of a story that didn't seem to belong to her anymore.

Carter sat beside her, his presence solid and steady, but there was a distance between them now. It wasn't the physical space—he was so close, his body almost touching hers—but something else. A subtle shift that neither of them could ignore. The quiet hum of tension filled the air, thick and suffocating.

He reached out, his hand hovering near hers, but he didn't touch her. Not yet. It was as if he, too, could feel it—the chasm between them that neither words nor touch seemed to bridge.

"Anastasia," Carter whispered, his voice rough, threaded with something darker. "Talk to me. Please."

She closed her eyes, a single tear slipping down her cheek before she could stop it. She wiped it away quickly, but the sensation lingered—like a crack in her chest she couldn't mend. She wanted to say something, to explain the coldness that had taken root inside her, but the words felt wrong. How could she explain it? How could she tell him that, despite everything, she felt like she was slowly fading away?

"I don't know what's happening anymore," she finally said, her voice barely audible. The confession was a release, but it didn't feel like a relief. "It's like... everything I thought I knew is unraveling. Like you're slipping through my fingers like I'm losing you to a story that I can't control."

Carter's breath caught, and she could see the way his jaw tightened as if he wanted to say something—anything—but the words wouldn't come. He reached for her again, his fingers brushing against hers, but there was something so fragile about the touch, something tentative.

"I'm right here," he said, his voice breaking in a way that made her heart twist. "You're not losing me, Anastasia. You're not."

But his words didn't quite reach her. Not fully. The space between them wasn't just physical—it was in the way his eyes searched hers as if trying to find something that wasn't there. It was in the way he touched her, hesitant, careful, like he was afraid she might disappear if he moved too quickly.

"I feel like I'm losing myself," she admitted, her voice cracking as the weight of it pressed down on her. "I don't know what's real anymore. Is this real, Carter? Are we real? Or am I just another part of some twisted story, something written in a book that's not even mine?"

Carter was silent for a long moment, his hand still hovering near hers, the space between them thick with unspoken words. He leaned forward, his forehead gently resting against hers, and she could feel the warmth of him, the steady rhythm of his heartbeat. But even that couldn't chase away the cold that had settled deep inside her.

"Anastasia," he whispered, his voice low and urgent, like he was trying to pull her back from the edge. "I don't know what's going on in your head, but I know this. What we have—*what we are*—it's real. You're real. I'm real. And I'm not going anywhere. Do you understand me?"

She wanted to believe him. She wanted to throw herself into him, let him pull her back into the warmth of his arms, back into something that made sense. But there was a part of her—small and quiet—that couldn't shake the fear that this was all slipping through her fingers. The doubt was too loud, too persistent.

"I wish I could believe you," she whispered, the words cutting her more than she expected. "But I don't know how."

For a moment, there was nothing but the soft sound of their breathing and the quiet tick of the clock in the corner of the room. And then, slowly, Carter's hand closed around hers, pulling her toward him, urging her into his arms. She let him because there was nothing left to do.

And yet, even as he held her close, as the warmth of his body enveloped hers, the space between them—the space in her heartfelt wider than it ever had before.

"I don't know how to fix this," she said, her voice muffled against his chest.

"I don't think we can fix it," Carter replied softly, his fingers threading through her hair, holding her like he was afraid she might slip away. "But we can try. We can keep trying."

She closed her eyes, letting herself be held, letting herself believe—just for a moment—that he was right. That they could keep trying. But deep down, there was something else, something cold that she couldn't shake: a quiet, lingering feeling that they were both lost in a world they could no longer control.

And the space between them—between what was real and what wasn't—only grew wider.

You feel it too, don't you?

The words whispered through her mind, just as they always did, like a ghostly reminder that she was still a character, still being watched. It was always there, lurking at the edges of the story.

But for now, she let herself stay in his arms. She let herself *believe* because even if everything around them was falling apart, she couldn't let go. Not yet.

Not until she had to.

One Last Chance

The air between them was thick with tension, each breath a fragile thing, teetering on the edge of breaking. Carter sat on the edge of the bed, hands clasped tightly together, his knuckles white from the pressure. He had tried everything—every word, every touch, every attempt to pull her back. But the distance between them was vast, a chasm neither of them had ever wanted to cross. It wasn't just physical; it was something deeper, something intangible, like they were two separate stories, written on different pages.

Anastasia stood by the window, her gaze fixed on the dark city skyline, but her mind was elsewhere. She didn't know where she was anymore—caught between what was real and what wasn't, wondering if everything she thought she knew was nothing more than a fractured illusion. She didn't even know if she could trust herself anymore, let alone Carter.

"I don't know how much longer I can keep pretending," she said softly, her voice carrying more weight than she intended. The words felt like a confession like she was admitting something she didn't want to face.

Carter looked up, his eyes dark with emotion—concern, frustration, fear. He had been trying so hard, doing everything in his power to fix things, but nothing seemed to reach her. Nothing seemed to get through the wall she had built around herself. And it was breaking him, piece by piece.

He stood up, walking toward her slowly, as if afraid that any sudden movement would send her further away. When he reached her, he stopped, just close enough to feel her warmth but far enough that it felt like a world between them.

"Anastasia," he began, his voice raw, almost pleading. "Please, look at me."

She turned to him then, her eyes clouded with doubt. "I *am* looking at you," she replied, but it was more of an accusation than a statement. The sadness in her voice cut deeper than any words he had ever heard. "But you're not here. Not really. You're not the person I thought you were. You're not even real. None of this is real, Carter."

The words hit him like a physical blow, the weight of them almost knocking the air from his lungs. He took a step closer, his hand reaching for hers, but she pulled back instinctively, as though his touch would burn her.

"I'm *real*, Anastasia," he said, his voice trembling with the desperation that had been building inside him for weeks. "I'm right here. I'm trying to fix this. *Please* let me fix this."

She closed her eyes, the tears that had been threatening to spill finally breaking free. "I don't know if I can believe you anymore," she whispered, her voice barely audible. "I don't know if I can believe in anything anymore."

Carter's chest tightened at the words, but he didn't give up. He couldn't. This was the last chance he had, the last time he could make her believe in him, in them. He wouldn't let her slip away. Not like this. Not when he had come this far.

He stepped forward, his hand gently cupping her cheek, his thumb brushing away the tears that had gathered there. She flinched slightly but didn't pull away. He held her gaze, trying to convey everything he couldn't say with words.

"I know I can't change the past," he murmured. "I know I can't erase the doubt in your heart, or the fear that's eating away at you. But I need you to believe me when I say this: I am here. And I'm not going anywhere."

Anastasia's breath hitched as she stared at him, her chest tight with the weight of everything she was feeling. But the doubt was still there, hanging like a cloud between them, threatening to pull them apart once again.

"You don't understand," she whispered, shaking her head. "I don't know what's real anymore. How can I trust anything when everything feels like a lie?"

Carter's heart ached at her words, but he refused to give up. This was his last chance. His final shot at saving them.

"Trust me," he said, his voice firm but gentle. "Trust *us*. I know this is hard, I know it feels like we're being torn apart, but we can fix this. You don't have to go through this alone."

For a moment, Anastasia just stood there, her eyes searching his, looking for something she wasn't sure she could find. And then, as if a switch had been flipped, she let out a long, shaky breath and closed the distance between them.

Before he could react, she threw her arms around him, her body trembling as she clung to him like he was the only thing keeping her grounded in a world that was unraveling.

Carter held her tightly, his hands running through her hair, whispering soft reassurances in her ear, anything to make her believe that they were still *real*—that this was still real. But as she pressed her face against his chest, he couldn't shake the feeling that something was still slipping away. The world around them, the story they were in, was unraveling faster than either of them could keep up with.

But for now, all he could do was hold her.

Because this was the last chance he had.

And he wasn't going to let go.

Not yet.

Carter held her, but as the seconds stretched into minutes, the silence between them grew thicker, heavier, like it had its weight. The tension in the air was palpable, suffocating, a reminder that despite the warmth of their embrace, something was *wrong*. Something was slipping through their fingers.

Anastasia's breathing was shallow, her chest rising and falling with the uncertainty that still gripped her. He could feel the way her body trembled as if it wasn't just the fear of their relationship falling apart that made her shake, but the overwhelming sense that *everything* around them was unraveling. She pulled back just slightly, but enough for Carter to feel the shift, the way the air between them thickened. She wasn't ready to let go, but she wasn't all in either.

"I don't know if I can do this," she whispered, her voice barely audible as if the weight of her words was too much to bear. Her eyes met his, searching, but not quite seeing him. It was as if she was looking beyond him, into the shadows that seemed to loom just out of sight, threatening to pull her away from him. "I don't know if I can trust you... or myself. Or anything anymore."

Carter's heart clenched, the pain of her words cutting through him like a blade. He wanted to reach out, to hold her closer, but he was terrified that if he moved wrong, she would slip through his fingers once more. The fear of losing her, of losing everything they had fought for, was too much.

"You *can* trust me," he said, his voice low but firm. "I'm right here. I'm *real*, Anastasia. *We* are real."

But the doubt lingered in her eyes, a flicker of something just beneath the surface that made Carter's pulse race. She was struggling with something he couldn't fully understand—something deeper than just him, deeper than their love. Something that felt like it was pulling her away from him.

The silence stretched, long and suffocating, before she finally spoke again, her words like a dagger to his chest.

"I don't know what's real anymore," she whispered. "I feel like I'm *not* even in control of this story. Like... like I'm just a character in a book, and someone else is writing the next page."

The words hung in the air between them, their weight almost too much to bear. Carter froze, staring at her, unsure of how to respond. There was a part of him that wanted to tell her she was imagining things, that everything was fine—that *they* were fine. But something in her eyes, something in the way she spoke, told him this wasn't just paranoia. This wasn't something she could easily shake off.

"You're not just a character," he said, his voice trembling with the force of his conviction. "You're *real*. You're *here*, with me. And I'm not going anywhere."

Her gaze flickered, uncertainty clouding her face again. She took a step back, her hands coming up to wrap around herself, as though she were trying to hold herself together. The distance between them felt so much wider now like the space between them had expanded into something insurmountable.

And then the feeling hit—suddenly, overwhelming. The sense that they were being watched. Not just by each other, but by *something else*. Something lurking at the edges of her mind, something that had always been there but was becoming impossible to ignore.

Anastasia's breath caught, and for a moment, she closed her eyes, as if bracing herself against the weight of it. "Do you feel that?" she whispered, her voice barely audible. "Like we're not alone... like someone's watching us?"

Carter's chest tightened, his pulse quickening. He didn't answer immediately, because he felt it too—a suffocating presence in the room, something hovering just outside the walls of their fragile reality. He had tried to ignore it, tried to push it away, but now that she had mentioned it, it was all he could focus on.

He reached for her again, his hand hovering near her shoulder, but she flinched, stepping away from him just enough to make him hesitate. His heart raced in his chest, but he held his ground, trying to keep the panic from creeping into his voice. "We're okay," he said, though the uncertainty in his own words was clear. "We're together. That's all that matters. And I swear I won't let anyone take you from me."

But as his words hung in the air, a flicker of something—something far beyond the walls of the room—brushed against their consciousness. It was as if the very fabric of their world had shifted, leaving them suspended between two realities. The line between what was real and what wasn't was blurring. And neither of them knew how much longer they could hold on.

Anastasia shook her head, her voice barely above a whisper. "I want to believe you. I *do*. But I feel like I'm... like I'm drowning in something I can't escape. Every time I think I'm pulling myself back, I'm pulled under again."

Carter could feel her slipping through his fingers—he could almost *see* it, the way her grip on reality was faltering. The fear of losing her, of watching her disappear into something he couldn't control, gripped him tighter than ever before.

"Anastasia, please," he whispered, desperation creeping into his voice. "This is our chance. Please, don't let go. I'm here. I'm *real*."

Her gaze met his, but it was distant, like she was seeing him from far away, through a haze of confusion and fear. And for a brief, terrifying moment, Carter wondered if it was already too late—if they had already crossed the point of no return.

But as the shadows seemed to stretch and pull at her, threatening to swallow her whole, Carter made a choice. He stepped forward, closing the distance between them, his hands grasping her shoulders, holding her in place.

"We're in this together," he said, his voice breaking with raw emotion. "I won't lose you. Not like this. Not to whatever's trying to tear us apart."

The tension between them crackled, and for a heartbeat, Anastasia didn't move. Then, slowly, her hand reached for him and the smallest spark of hope flickered in his chest.

But it wasn't enough. Not yet.

The presence, the feeling of being watched—it was still there. The walls of their world were closing in, and Carter knew deep down that their fragile connection wasn't enough to protect them from what was coming. The story they were living in, the one they thought they could control, was unraveling, and neither of them knew how much time they had left.

But as Anastasia's fingers curled into his, Carter's resolve hardened.

If this was their last chance, he would fight for it. He would fight for them—no matter the cost.

And yet, with every passing second, the space between them—between what they were and what they could be—grew larger. And somewhere, in the back of their minds, they both knew it was only a matter of time before everything came crashing down.

And they might not survive the fall.

The Final Page

The room was quieter than it had been in weeks, the silence settling over them like a blanket. Everything had changed—everything had shifted. Anastasia felt as though she had crossed a threshold, a line she had been waiting to step over for what felt like a lifetime. But now, standing on the other side, she felt different. Stronger. Finally free.

Carter stood beside her, his hand resting gently on her shoulder, a touch that was grounding and comforting all at once. They had fought for this moment—for *this* life—and now that it was here, the world felt lighter, as though the heavy weight of the past had finally been lifted.

Her parents were sitting in the living room, just a few steps away, watching the two of them with a quiet pride in their eyes. Anastasia could hardly believe they were here, that she was standing in the same room with them after everything that had happened—the fears, the doubts, the battles they had fought, and the curse that had loomed over her like a dark cloud. But now, it was gone. All of it.

Her mother's eyes met hers from across the room, a smile spreading across her face, warm and full of love. Her father, ever the quiet protector, simply nodded, his gaze full of approval. They had witnessed her struggle, seen her break and rebuild herself, and now they could finally see the daughter they had always hoped for—the one they had loved even in her darkest moments.

The air in the room had changed. There was no more fear, no more uncertainty. Only the softness of a new beginning. A chance to finally live, to move forward, without the weight of the past holding them back.

Anastasia turned to Carter, her heart swelling with emotion, and for the first time in what felt like forever, she saw him—not just as the man she loved, but as her partner, the person who had walked beside her through it all. The person who had never given up, even when everything seemed impossible.

Her hand reached up to gently touch his cheek, her fingers trembling slightly from the sheer magnitude of the moment. "We did it," she whispered, her voice thick with emotion.

Carter's lips curved into a smile, but there was something deeper in his eyes—something that spoke of relief, of shared triumph. "We did," he replied softly, his voice rough with the weight of the words. "Together."

Anastasia felt the tears welling in her eyes—tears of joy, of everything they had fought for. She had believed in them, in their love, even when it felt like they were fighting against the world itself. And now, here they were, standing on the other side, hand in hand, free.

And as if the universe itself was allowing them this final moment of peace, Carter stepped closer, his hand sliding into hers, his gaze never leaving hers. The room seemed to fade around them, the sounds of the world outside becoming distant. It was just them now—just the two of them and the love they had fought so hard to protect.

"Anastasia," Carter murmured, his voice a soft caress against the stillness of the moment. "I never thought we'd get here. But now that we are... I can't imagine living in any world without you."

Her heart raced at his words, the weight of his love settling deep within her. She had felt his heart, had seen his struggles, and now, with every part of her being, she knew they were exactly where they were meant to be.

Without another word, Carter leaned in, and she met him halfway, her lips finding him in a kiss that was gentle at first—tentative, as if they were both savoring the sweetness of the moment. But then, as the kiss deepened, it became something more—a promise, a declaration. A love that had withstood everything, and now, nothing could tear them apart.

As they pulled away, breathless, Anastasia's eyes locked with his, and in that moment, she saw it. The future. Their future. It was finally theirs to claim.

Behind them, her parents were watching, but Anastasia didn't need to look. She could feel their support, their love, their acceptance. And it was enough. She had broken the curse and fought for her happiness, and now, she was ready to start her life—no longer bound by anything but love.

"I love you, Carter," she whispered, her voice filled with everything she had never been able to say before.

"I love you, too," he replied, his voice filled with a quiet strength. "Always."

And as they stood there, wrapped in each other's arms, the final page of their story turned—no longer filled with fear or doubt, but with the promise of a new beginning. The curse was broken. The darkness had lifted. And in the light of their love, they had found their happily ever after.

And this time, it was real.

The room around them seemed to fade into the background as they stood in the quiet comfort of each other's embrace. Outside, the world continues, but for Anastasia and Carter, time had paused, just for a moment, to let them breathe, to let them savor the sweetness of what they had won.

Carter's fingers gently brushed through her hair, pushing a stray lock behind her ear as he studied her face. There was a softness in his gaze that hadn't been there before, an openness, a certainty that spoke of everything they had survived. "We've made it," he whispered again, almost as if to convince himself as much as her.

Anastasia nodded, her hand resting over his heart, feeling the steady beat beneath her palm. It was a sound she had learned to love, a reminder that everything was real now—that their love, their future, was theirs to hold.

"We did," she said, her voice full of wonder as if the truth of it hadn't fully settled in. She had spent so much time fighting, questioning, wondering if things would ever turn around, but now, it was all clear. She felt *complete.*

Behind them, her parents—her *real* parents—were watching with tears in their eyes. Her mother, who had been there through every dark moment, every fear and hesitation, smiled softly at her, while her father, ever stoic, had the faintest glimmer of pride in his expression.

Anastasia turned to them, her heart full of gratitude, for everything they had given her. The love she had longed for from them, the acceptance, was here now, like a light they had waited to shine through the cracks.

Her mother stood first, her arms open wide, welcoming her back into the fold. "You're home, darling," she whispered, her voice thick with emotion. "You've been through so much, but now, you're finally free."

Anastasia felt her chest tighten, her throat swelling with emotion. "I didn't think it was possible," she confessed, stepping into her mother's embrace. "But... we're here. We're okay."

Her father, still a man of few words, placed his hand on her shoulder. "You always had it in you," he said, his voice deep and calm. "You just had to believe it. And I'm proud of you."

Tears filled Anastasia's eyes as she looked between them, the two people who had loved her, even when she felt lost, even when the darkness around her seemed too much to overcome. The family she had always wanted, was finally whole.

As Carter moved to her side, standing shoulder to shoulder with her, their hands naturally intertwined, Anastasia felt the weight of everything they had just conquered fall away. There were no more fears, no more shadows. Just love. Real love. And, for the first time in what felt like forever, hope. Hope for what would come next, for the life they would build together.

Anastasia turned to Carter, her eyes locking with his, the bond between them stronger than ever. She saw the future in his gaze—filled with light, filled with everything they had fought for. *Together*. The curse was gone, the past erased, and all that remained was the open road ahead.

"Do you remember," she began softly, her voice trembling, "when we thought we might lose each other? When everything seemed impossible?"

Carter nodded, squeezing her hand gently. "I remember. But I never stopped believing in us."

Anastasia smiled a slow, deep smile that reached her eyes. "Neither did I," she said, voice steady now, full of certainty. "And now... we get to write the rest of our story."

And for the first time, she didn't feel like a character in a book, her life dictated by forces beyond her control. She was *living* it—*writing* it. Each moment was theirs to claim, and they would claim it together.

With her parents in the background, the promise of a life full of love and freedom ahead of them, and Carter by her side, Anastasia felt as if the world had finally opened up to her. She wasn't just surviving anymore—she was living. She was whole.

Carter's lips met hers once more, a kiss that sealed everything they had been through and everything they would become. It was tender at first, a shared relief, a gentle reaffirmation of all they had fought for. But as it deepened, the passion surged—a fierce, desperate longing, a celebration of the life that was finally theirs. No more curses. No more doubts.

Just love.

And when they pulled away, breathless and smiling, Carter whispered against her lips, "I can't wait to spend forever with you."

Anastasia's heart fluttered at his words, the promise of forever wrapping around them like a cocoon, safe and certain. She pressed her forehead to his, smiling through her tears, and whispered back, "Forever sounds perfect."

Behind them, her parents shared a quiet, knowing look. There were no more curses to break. No more battles to fight. Only the joy of watching their daughter embrace the life she had always deserved.

And as Anastasia and Carter stood together, ready to face whatever the future held, they knew this was the beginning of something beautiful. Their story had reached its final page—and yet, somehow, it felt as if it was only just beginning.

A love so strong, so true, could never truly end.

And in that moment, under the warm, golden glow of the life they had built, they kissed once more—proof that no matter what came next, their love would always be real.

And that, in the end, was enough...

As they stood in the quiet after their kiss, the world outside continued, unchanged, but everything inside the walls of their home felt transformed. The sun had begun to dip below the horizon, casting a soft golden light through the window, bathing the room in warmth. For the first time in what felt like a lifetime, Anastasia felt truly at peace.

Carter's hand found hers again, his fingers lacing through hers with the same familiarity they had always shared, but now with a deeper, more knowing connection. They stood there, together, as if trying to memorize this moment, as if they both knew how fragile it had once seemed—and how strong it was now.

Her parents had settled into the background, giving them space, but there was no mistaking the pride and love in their eyes. Anastasia caught her mother's gaze one last time, seeing the way her mother's eyes shimmered with unshed tears, and she felt an overwhelming surge of gratitude.

"Are you happy?" Carter asked quietly, pulling her gaze back to him. His voice was soft, tentative as if he needed to hear her say it out loud, needed to hear that all their struggles, all their pain, had been worth it.

Anastasia smiled, her heart full as she met his gaze. "I am," she whispered, her voice a steady certainty. "I'm more than happy. I'm... I'm home."

Carter's smile widened, and there was a spark of something fierce in his eyes. "And you always will be," he promised. "No matter what."

Anastasia nodded, squeezing his hand. "I believe you."

They stood there for a few more moments, their hearts still racing from the emotions of the day, from the sheer weight of everything that had shifted in the last hours. And in that peaceful, quiet moment, with their hands intertwined, they knew that they had done it—*together*.

The storm had passed. The curse was broken. And there was nothing but the bright future before them.

Anastasia looked back at her parents, who had quietly returned to their seats, exchanging knowing glances. Her mother gave her a small, approving nod, and for the first time in a long time, Anastasia felt she had fully earned their love. It had been so much more than the curse—so much more than the darkness she had been trapped in. It had always been about finding her place in the world. Finding the love and acceptance she had been searching for her whole life.

And now, here she was, standing in the light, surrounded by the people she loved.

Carter leaned down, pressing his lips to her forehead. "Whatever comes next, we'll face it together. Always."

Anastasia smiled up at him, her heart swelling with love, with a sense of peace she had never felt before. "Together," she agreed softly.

And as the sun set, casting a soft golden light over their world, Anastasia knew that this was only the beginning. With Carter, with her family, she had everything she needed to build the life they had always dreamed of.

And this time, she would write the pages of her own story—one where love conquered all, and where nothing could ever tear them apart again.

Epilogue

The wind whispered through the trees outside, carrying with it the scent of fresh rain, the kind of rain that washed away everything—every trace of dust, every bit of darkness. The world felt different now. It felt lighter, freer. Anastasia stood at the window of their home, her gaze lost in the soft, amber light of the setting sun, her hand resting gently on the glass as if she could somehow hold the moment there, forever.

It had been months since the curse had been broken. Since that night—when the world seemed to shift and realign, and everything she thought she knew about herself, about love, had been rewritten.

But now, as the seasons changed, so had she. So had they.

She looked over her shoulder, her heart swelling in her chest as her eyes met Carter's. He was sitting on the couch, a book in his hands, but his focus was entirely on her, as it always was. They had built a life together—slowly, carefully, but with certainty. Every day, they wove themselves into each other's lives more and more. It wasn't perfect—nothing ever truly was—but it was theirs. And for the first time, she knew it was real.

Her parents had been there, too, in ways that neither of them had expected. The relationship they had once struggled with, strained and fractured, had healed over time, as all things did. Her mother had become the pillar she had always longed for, offering advice and understanding, while her father, though still quiet, was a steady presence in her life. Together, as a family, they had grown stronger. They had found their way back to each other.

Anastasia felt something stir within her, a sense of peace that had been elusive for so long. She didn't need to search anymore. She had found her place.

Turning back to Carter, she walked over to him, the softness in her steps matching the stillness of the room. He smiled up at her, a smile that spoke of years of shared laughter, of moments that were quiet but full of meaning.

"Come sit with me," he said, setting the book aside and pulling her gently down next to him on the couch. His arm wrapped around her, and she nestled into him, the familiar comfort of his touch anchoring her.

"I was thinking about everything we've been through," she said softly, her fingers tracing small circles on the back of his hand. "How we didn't know what was real, how everything felt like it was slipping away."

Carter's thumb brushed over her knuckles, a silent promise that no matter the past, they had created something indestructible together. "But we fought for it. We fought for each other," he murmured. "That was real. Everything else? It's just noise."

Anastasia smiled, leaning her head on his shoulder. "I never thought I could love someone this much. After everything... the curse, the fear, all of it. But now, I know that it was always going to be us."

"It always was," he agreed, kissing the top of her head. "And it always will be."

The weight of everything they had endured settled in her chest, but this time it was not with bitterness or fear. It was with gratitude. They had been broken—but now they were whole. The curse was no longer something that controlled them, something that had haunted her since the very beginning. They had faced it together, had overcome it, and now, they had built a future.

A future where love had triumphed.

Anastasia's eyes fluttered shut, her heart beating steadily as she listened to the rhythm of their breaths as if the world outside had faded entirely. There was no more darkness, no more ghosts lingering in the corners of their lives. Just the warmth of the love they shared, growing stronger with each passing day.

For the first time in a long time, Anastasia allowed herself to believe in the beauty of the life they had built—a life without fear, without uncertainty. A life full of love, laughter, and a peace she had once thought impossible.

When she finally opened her eyes, Carter was watching her with a quiet smile. He seemed to know, somehow, exactly what was in her heart. He always did.

And as the last rays of the sun disappeared behind the horizon, leaving only the quiet embrace of twilight, she realized that this was exactly where she was meant to be. Not just here, in this moment, but in every moment that followed. With him.

She shifted, turning in his arms, and as their lips met in a kiss that was slow and soft, Anastasia knew that their story—*their* story—wasn't over. It had just begun. And whatever came next, they would face it together.

No curses. No illusions. Just love.

And that, she realized, was more than enough.

Finally, I had a normal morning again unless...

The end.